Camilla is an engineer the whimsical realm of r........

She writes contemporary rom-coms. Her characters have big hearts, might be a little stubborn at times, and love to banter with each other. Every story she pens has a guaranteed HEA that will make your heart beat faster. Unless you're a vampire, of course.

Camilla is a cat lover, coffee addict, and shoe hoarder. Besides writing, she loves reading—duh!—cooking, watching bad TV, and going to the movies—popcorn, please. She's a bit of a foodie, nothing too serious. A keen traveler, Camilla knows mosquitoes play a vital role in the ecosystem, and she doesn't want to starve all those frog princes out there, but she could really live without them.

You can find out more about her here: **www.camillaisley.com** and by following her on Instagram or Facebook.

By the Same Author

CAMILLA ISLEY

Home for Christmas

Dedication

To all vacation mishap sufferers, may something good come out of your misfortunes…

One

Wendy

"Christmas is ruined!" my sister declares over the phone the moment I pick up.

"Hold on a second," I say, moving away from the stage so as not to disturb the rehearsal. From Amy's dramatic opening, I've got a feeling this conversation is going to take a while.

The notes of the main theme song fill the theater before I can get to the dressing rooms area, and my sister asks, "Are you at work?"

"Yes, Amy, it's what people do on a Wednesday morning."

"Not you, you usually live like a vampire: write at night and avoid the light of day at all costs."

I meander down a narrow corridor, zigzagging among dancers stretching against the walls. "That's when I'm writing, but today's the last rehearsal before opening night on Friday. I sent you the tickets, didn't I?"

"Yes, yes! Sorry, I'm sleep deprived and scatterbrained. But Friday night is the light at the end of the tunnel. Thank goodness! Trevor booked the babysitter like a month ago and he also has a replacement lined up in case Jodie bails on us at the last minute. We need a night away from the twins. And nothing beats having tickets to 'the most anticipated, sold-out-for-months, Broadway musical of the season,'" Amy says, quoting an article that came out in the *New York Times* last weekend.

I smile as I finally reach my tiny office on the theater's lower level. I shut myself in and sit behind the ancient wooden desk. *Forgotten Dreams* is the first musical I've written that has been produced. It's going to make or break my career. The marketing team has done a stellar job building the hype, but until I read an actual good review, I'll be a bundle of nerves.

"You're welcome," I say.

"Are you free to talk?" Amy asks, her voice turning anxious again.

"Yes," I say. "They're still rehearsing the choreographies. I'm not needed. Why is Christmas ruined?"

"Oh, Wendy, Mom has lost it. She's saying she doesn't want to host Christmas this year."

"Has she given you a reason?"

"Yeah, she claims she's too old to cook for ten people."

I do a mental indexing of our family. There's me and my boyfriend, Brandon, and that makes two. Joshua, our younger brother, three. Mom, four. Amy and her husband, five and six. Their two older kids bring us up to eight. But ten? "Is Mom counting the twins as eating guests?" I ask aloud. "Did you tell her making a bottle of milk doesn't count as cooking?"

"Yes, I did. She's using it as an excuse. The situation is serious. She's even refusing to put decorations around the house."

"Why?"

"Because then they'd just have to go back in a box after a month and what a waste of her time that would be."

"Okay, I get it."

"No, Wendy, she said she doesn't want a Christmas tree."

"The decorations, the tree… all things Dad used to do," I say, thinking Mom loves Christmas, and we've spent the day at her house for as long as I can remember. December 25th has always been her favorite day of the year, at least while Dad was with us. "Could that be why she's rejecting all those traditions?" I ask.

"Of course. What else could it be? Mom lost the love of her life and she's heartbroken, but it's no reason to cancel Christmas. I'm sad, too, Dad is gone, but this is also the twins' first Christmas and I was looking forward to it."

I grab a pencil and doodle candy canes on the front page of the *Forgotten Dreams* script. "What if we cooked everything, brought the food to her house, and cleaned up afterward?"

"Wendy, you can't boil an egg."

"Well, okay. But I could be your scullery maid and clean all the pots and pans after you've cooked and tackle some basic tasks like peeling potatoes. And Joshua could take care of the tree and the decorations. He should get off school in time to set up the house."

"I offered to cook, but she said she doesn't want to spend Christmas in, I quote, *that house.*"

"Okay, that makes sense. I'm not saying I'm happy about not spending Christmas at home, but I can see her point. The house is still full of Dad. They spent a lifetime there together. The memories might be too hard to endure at the holidays." I add a broken heart to my drawing. "What if we did it at your house? I'd offer my apartment, but my dinner table wouldn't fit half of us."

"Mom says she doesn't want to be in New York at all."

"But what's the alternative?"

"She says she wants to take a family vacation."

"To go where?"

"She tried to suggest we go on a cruise to the Caribbean, but that's where I dug my feet in. If we have to spend the holidays in some random place, I want to go somewhere wintery, with snow."

"That isn't such a bad idea. I haven't gone skiing in forever. We could make it a family vacation, like old times when we all still lived at home."

"Except we never went at Christmas."

"What did Joshua say?"

"I haven't called him yet," Amy says. "I wanted to talk to you first."

I draw snowy mountain peaks. "I bet he'd be on board with a ski trip."

"Yeah, pity we're never going to find a decent place with only three weeks to go before the holidays."

"Let's have a look first, and despair later. Mindy might be able to help," I say, referring to my best friend and also the best travel agent in the city. "If someone can make the impossible happen, it's her."

I hang up with my sister and speed-dial Mindy.

She picks up on the third ring. "Wendy?"

"Hello, how is my favorite person and best travel agent in the world?"

"Why do I have a feeling you're about to unload one of your 'when hell freezes over' requests on me?" she accuses.

"Can't I just call my best friend to say hi with no hidden agenda?"

"Not when it's opening week for the most important play you've ever worked on and you must be neck-deep into the last rehearsal."

"Okay," I confess. "I need a favor."

"From your tone, you sound more like you need a miracle. Shoot."

"Kinda," I say, and relate the mom drama. "In short, we need a cabin or a chalet somewhere nice and Christmassy with snow and a decent ski resort nearby that can accommodate Brandon and me, my mom, Joshua, Amy and her husband, and their four kids."

Mindy low-whistles. "Would you also like the moon?"

I bite on a fingernail. "That hard, uh? I promise the twins don't take up much space, they can sleep in the same room with Amy and Trevor."

"Still close to impossible, at least if the 'somewhere nice' and 'decent ski resort' parts are essential. Budget?"

"We're all pitching in, you should have some wiggle room."

"Okay, let me see what I can do, but I'm not making any promises. All right?"

"I'm sure you'll find us the perfect solution." Just then, an announcement for all the actors to convene to the main stage comes over the theater speaker system. "Listen, I have to go now."

"Yeah, I heard. Talk soon."

We hang up, and I hop up the stairs two at a time, filled with optimism. After the grim Christmas we spent at the hospital last year, days away from Dad's passing, a family vacation is exactly what we need to find our holiday cheer again.

Before opening the door to the stage, I stop. I should probably inform my boyfriend I'm planning a vacation for us. Brandon hates it when I call him in the middle of the workday, so I shoot him a text instead.

Hey, what would you say about a ski trip over Christmas?

Like a weekend thing?

More a week

My whole family is going

A week? I might as well tell my boss I don't care about making partner.

Sorry, babe, no can do

My heart sinks, even if his reply didn't come as a total surprise. In the almost two years we've been dating, Brandon's job has always taken precedence over our relationship.

When I met him in a bar in downtown Manhattan, his commitment to his career was one of his selling points. He looked dashing in a dark suit with his tie half undone and his shirt sleeves rolled up. And I was more than ready to move past the artist types I'd serial dated for years. Mostly broke dudes who spent their days being "creative." Which meant they either slept or drank or got high. The type of guy who thought money was a dirty word.

Guess falling for an investment banker turned the tables on that attitude.

I shrug as I put my phone away before re-entering the theater. Brandon or not, it's still going to be the best family holiday ever.

Two

Riven

Preacher grabbed the guide rope, the straw coarse in his hands, and went groping down the passage on all fours. Doubts coiled around his soul just as the rope did around his wrist. What would await them out of the tunnel? Would it be any better than the mercenaries they were trying to escape? If they made it out at all.

Wyatt moaned behind him, the sound bouncing off the tight walls in a sinister echo. Preacher looked back. The faint halo of his flashlight cast a shadow on his partner's figure slouched on the floor. Wyatt had lost too much blood. If they wanted to make it out of the caves alive, forward was the only way.

Bzzzzzz. Bzzzz. Bzzzzz.

I tear my eyes away from the computer screen and curse at the phone. I forgot to turn it off and left it on the kitchen counter. Rookie mistake. I ignore the buzzing noise and go back to my manuscript.

Forward was the only way... and...

Nothing. The flow of words is lost. Whatever brilliant segue I was about to write has escaped my brain.

I bang a frustrated fist on the dining table and stand up. I might as well check who the bugger is.

Tess, my sister.

I know what the call is about, and I have zero patience for the guilt-tripping right now.

With the phone in my hand, I lean against the kitchen counter and stare out the giant French window in the living room. The sun is shining on the tall mountain peaks covered in snow. The slopes will open soon, and I would like nothing better than to take my snowboard and join the tourists on a black run. But today I won't allow myself to go outside until I've met my word count. No matter that by lunchtime, the terrain on the slopes will be either mushy, hard packed, or scattered around in impromptu moguls. I sigh as I imagine the pristine white blanket it must be now and close my eyes regretfully. Not today.

The phone stops vibrating. Will Tess give up after one call?

Bzzzzzz. Bzzzz. Bzzzzz. The buzzing resumes at once.

Nope.

If I ignore her, she'll just keep pestering me. And even if I turned off the phone, the shadow of the difficult conversation would loom over my head as my Sword of Damocles.

Resigned, I pick up. "Hell—"

"Dad says you're not coming home for Christmas," Tess interrupts me.

"Well, no one could accuse you of not being direct."

"Is it true?"

"Yes."

"Why? Life has given you lemons this past year, agreed, but it's no excuse to skip Christmas."

"Tess, I have a deadline and I'm already behind. The last thing I need is to waste time booking flights, checking in and out of airports to fly home for just a day."

"Then stay longer. You've been holed up in that cabin for months. I haven't seen you since, mmm—"

The words she's looking for are: since you announced your wife was leaving you for a C-list soap opera celebrity mere days after you'd started a complete remodeling of your house, which is now a construction site you cannot either sell or live in.

"Yeah," I say. "It's been a minute."

"Come on, Riv, we never skipped Christmas. If I came back from my gap year in Sri Lanka, you can take a 90-minute flight home."

"Tess, I need to finish this book. I'm stuck."

"You've been up there forever. If you're still blocked after all this time, maybe a change of scenery will be good. Come on, it's Christmas."

I grab the counter with my free hand, knuckles going white. "Tess—"

"Dad is too decent to say anything, but I'm not. I'll never forgive you if you don't come home and use a stupid book as an excuse."

"It's not an excuse, I'm months behind."

"Riven Clark, I know you. You're using your unfinished novel as an alibi to play the hermit and avoid seeing everyone you know. Cassie pulled a number on you. She should be the one ashamed to show her face in public, not you."

I let go of the counter to massage my temple. The call is going worse than I expected.

"Please," Tess insists. "Please, please, pretty please, say you'll come home."

"Okay, I give up, you win!" Fighting her is going to cause me more stress than simply giving in.

"Yay, you'll have a blast at home, I promise. Oh, and Dad said you can stay with him, of course. I have to call him with the good news. Talk-later-love-ya-bye."

Tess hangs up before I can add anything, just as the doorbell rings. That's odd. It's early for the mailman.

I go to the door and find the town marshal standing on the porch.

"Morning, Marshal," I greet him. "What's going on?" I'm not used to receiving house visits from local law enforcement.

"Good day to you, too." He tips his hat at me. "Nasty business, I'm afraid. We have a rogue wolf on our hands. It sneaked up on old Ford last night while he was taking logs into the house and almost bit his leg off."

"Oh, gosh, wow." I rake a hand through my hair. "How is he?"

"They brought him down to Salt Lake Regional Medical Center; they say they should be able to save the leg."

"Is it normal for wolves to attack humans?"

"No, but we believe this is an old beast, shunned by its pack. It can't hunt in the wild alone, and it's getting desperate." The marshal pulls on his short beard. "I'm making rounds to the most isolated houses, asking residents to be extra careful, especially when they go out at night. Don't leave food waste around. And if you have to step out in the dead of night for whatever reason, at least carry a rifle."

"I wouldn't know what to do with it."

"Ah, I forgot they don't teach you fancy folks how to shoot in California. Well, if you ain't going to bring a gun, take an ax with you." He mimics the movement of swinging the weapon with his wrist. "Those are pretty intuitive."

An idea strikes me. What if Preacher encountered a wild beast in one of the caves? He wouldn't have an ax to defend himself, but he could use a knife. My mind swirls with the possibilities, the scene taking form in my head.

"Thank you," I say, eager to go back to my laptop. "I'll be extra careful and let you know if I hear any suspicious howling."

I say goodbye to the marshal and rush back to the computer, my fingers flying on the keyboard.

...Two blazing points of yellow-green flame shone with the reflected light of Preacher's flashlight bouncing off the stone walls. Preacher considered turning the light off, but that would only give the big cat the advantage of total darkness—of which he was the seeing master. No, Preacher secured the flashlight to the straps of his backpack and unsheathed the knife at his belt, ready to fight for his life...

Bzzzzzz. Bzzzz. Bzzzzz.

"Aaaargh," I scream in frustration.

With the marshal ringing at the door right after I hung up with my sister, I forgot to turn off the phone—*again!*

I get up ready to smash the damn thing and go incommunicado until Christmas, but then I see it's an unknown number calling—someone with a local area code. What now? A grizzly bear woke up early from hibernation and is targeting authors with writer's block?

I pick up. "Riven Clark."

"Hello, Mr. Clark, this is Kelly Anne from the Richter Real Estate Group," my real estate agent says in her adorable southern lilt.

"Hi, Kelly Anne," I say, surprised. I should have her number in my contacts. I stare at the screen to double-check. "Did you change your number?"

"No, sorry, I'm calling from my personal phone. Work one died."

"Oh, okay. What's up? Is there a problem with the rent? I'd planned to come into town later today to deposit my check."

"No, no, Mr. Clark, nothing like that. Stop by whenever it's most convenient for you. Today, tomorrow, there's no hurry. I was calling you for an entirely different reason. Am I catching you at a good time?"

No point in telling her she, my sister, and the town marshal are doing their best to disrupt my writing. "Sure," I say, and drop the phone on the counter, putting her on speaker. I need more coffee.

"Oh, great. You're booked at the cabin until April, of course, but I was wondering if you were going home for the holidays by any chance."

"As a matter of fact, I've just been strong-armed into making that decision by my sister," I reply. "Why?"

"How sweet, your family must really miss you." Kelly Anne chuckles. "And since you'll be gone, would you be interested in subletting the cabin for Christmas week? Park City is sold out this year. I can't believe the number of people we've had to turn down for the holidays." She chuckles again. "It's called peak season for a reason. Anyway, if you sublet the cabin, you could make all of April's rent back in a single week. Is that something you'd consider?"

I pour water into the coffee machine's tank and ponder for a second.

I'm not strapped for money by any standard, but saving a month's rent wouldn't be the worst thing, especially considering how much the renovations on the house are going to cost. Besides, Cassie will probably ask her lawyers to strip me of every last penny she can grab. "I could," I say, and add coffee to the filter. "But what about my stuff? I wouldn't want to leave my clothes around the cabin and have strangers poke through it."

"That wouldn't be a problem, Mr. Clark. One of my teams could pack everything for you and store it for the week, and of course, unpack before you come back. What dates were you planning to leave?"

"I haven't booked my flight out of Salt Lake City, yet." I pull up the calendar on my phone, looking at the dates. I could stretch my stay to a week and make everyone at home happy. Then they might back off a little and let me write in peace until Easter. "What if I left on the twenty-first and came back on the twenty-ninth? That would leave you a full week in the middle."

"That'd be perfect, Mr. Clark. I'll free those dates up on our calendar and I'll leave some papers for you to sign at the agency. You can formalize the agreement when you drop off your rent check."

"Okay, I'll come down as soon as I'm finished writing for the day."

"Take all the time you need, as I said, no hurry. Thanks so much and I'm looking forward to seeing you later."

We end the call, and I turn on the coffee maker.

As I watch the dark liquid drop into the pot, I try to mentally return to a dingy cave alongside Preacher, the treasure hunter hero of all my adventure novels.

In my mind, the trickle of the coffee transforms into dirty water seeping from the cave's ceiling and dropping, cold and chafing, down Preacher's collar as he and the beast circle each other in a dance of death.

Dance of death, that's good.

I have to type it before I forget. But this time, before I get back to my laptop, I turn off the phone.

Three

Wendy

The music stops as the two lead actors are about to kiss at the end of the first act, turning the theater so quiet you could hear a pin drop at the back of the room. So, when my phone starts vibrating on the staff table just off the stage, it sounds as loud as a bomb going off.

I look at the name on the screen: Mindy.

I grab the phone and excuse myself, whispering, "Sorry, family emergency. Carry on without me."

The director frowns at me, then, turning toward the actors, he swirls a finger in the air, shouting, "Scene, back from the start."

I rush out of the theater and pick up as soon as the main door closes behind me.

"I'm here," I say, out of breath.

"Woah," Mindy greets me. "What's with the panting? Have you opted for a career change and joined the backup dancers, or were you having a torrid affair with the sound manager and I interrupted?"

"No to the dancing, and no to the torrid affair. I had to run out before the director killed me for interrupting the scene rehearsal. And you know I'd never cheat on Brandon, or anyone else. Why the sound manager, anyway?"

"I don't know. It seemed like someone cool to have an affair with. Don't they get their own booth where you two could have crazy sex on the control board and then you'd accidentally turn on the microphone switch with your bum and suddenly the entire cast would hear you make guttural

16

sounds?"

I blink. "You watch too much TV. And the sound director is fifty."

"Ah, bet he might teach you a trick or two."

I shake my head. "You're impossible." I walk a few paces away from the doors to make sure no one hears my "family emergency" and ask, "Please tell me you have good news for me?"

"I searched for a vacancy on ski resorts all over the country, and they're all booked solid for Christmas—"

"But," I interrupt. "There must be a 'but' at the end of that phrase."

"Buuut... just as I was checking my favorite agency in Park City, a spot magically opened. Christmas week went from red to green under my eyes. But it won't stay green for long, so I'm going to give you all the facts pronto. The house is a refurbished cabin in the woods about fifteen minutes from the town's center with very cozy, mountain-chic decor. The downside: it only has four bedrooms. Amy and Trevor could sleep in the master with the twins. Then there are two singles, one for your mom, and the other has a full bed that might fit you and Brandon if you want to hug tight at night—"

"Brandon can't come, so that isn't an issue."

"Let me guess, work?" Mindy asks.

I roll my eyes and bite my tongue. I'm not in the mood for one of her your-boyfriend-doesn't-value-you-enough pep talks. "What about the fourth room?"

"It has a bunk bed that would be perfect for the older kids."

"And Joshua?"

"That's the thing, he'd have to sleep on the sofa bed in the living room."

"Mmm. Where is Park City, anyway?"

"Utah."

"Utah? That's like super far."

"Beggars can't be choosers," Mindy sing-songs. "I'm telling you, this is your only option, and if you don't book it fast, it'll be gone before lunchtime."

"The town is nice?"

"Very quaint, with old storefronts and cozy restaurants, but also some gourmet options if you decide to go foodie. And the location is perfect, right in the middle of a few of the best ski resorts in the country: Park City, Alta, Deer Valley, Park City Mountain... you can try a different one each day if you want."

"Okay, I'm sold, book it. Could you also sort the plane tickets? Five adults, two kids, and the twins, but they don't pay yet, right?"

"Sure, I'm going to need a copy of everyone's IDs. And I guess you'll also want a couple of rental cars to move around once you get to Utah."

"Yes, yes, those too."

"Or would you prefer a minivan that can fit the whole gang?"

I consider for a second. "No, better do the two cars so we can split if people want to do different activities."

"Perfect." I can practically see Mindy seated at her minimalistic desk, taking notes as we speak. "To recap, one cabin, nine plane tickets, two cars, and four car seats? Or are Vicky and Owen old enough to go without one?"

"No, yeah, Amy still uses car seats for them."

"Four car seats it is, then. Your family vacation is so *Home Alone* I want to gag."

"Nah, come on, in *Home Alone* they had at least ten kids, we only have four."

And if Brandon keeps being so career centered, I'm afraid we won't be adding to that tally anytime soon.

"All right," Mindy says. "The house is booked."

Four

Riven

Three solid hours of writing later, I crack my neck as I look away from the computer screen for the first time. Outside, the sun is already descending over the mountains while still shining brightly. I check my watch: two-thirty. My stomach growls in response.

I pat my belly. "Yep, it's past our lunchtime, buddy."

I could grab a burger at the local pub before I drop by the rental agency and catch two birds with one stone.

I snatch the car keys from a bowl on the kitchen island and, as an afterthought, pick up my phone as well. As I turn it on, it buzzes with a million notifications, mostly from my sister.

I have half a mind to ignore her and not call her back until later tonight. I already agreed to go home. What else could she want? But then I find a missed call also from my dad. He never calls unless something is up—*he,* contrary to everybody else in my family, understands why I had to get away from LA and how important my writing time is.

I call Dad back first, but he doesn't pick up. With a sigh, I tap Tess's contact next.

She answers on the first ring. "Where were you? Why was your phone off? I've been trying to call you for hours."

I was WRITING!!! I want to scream. They all assume that since I can work from home at any hour of the day, my job doesn't warrant the same respect or boundaries of a nine-to-five desk gig. I bite down my retort and ask instead, "Has something happened? Is Dad okay?"

"Yeah, he is. But his house isn't."

"Why? What happened?"

"Busted pipe. I just came back from Dad's and it's a disaster. The lower floor is flooded. The contractor said he has to replace all the pipes, break the floors, the walls—it's going to take weeks."

"Where's Dad staying?"

"With us. The kids will bunk together for a few weeks but we can't have Christmas dinner at our place. Our house isn't big enough. Did you already book your flight to come home?"

"No," I say. "Are you telling me *not* to? I thought the Clarks couldn't skip Christmas."

"And we can't, but what if we came to you? The cabin is huge, right? It'd fit us."

I make a quick count of the bedrooms. If I leave the master for Tess and her husband, Dad and I can each sleep in one of the singles, and Tess's kids can sleep in the bunk beds. But what about Skeeter, our younger brother?

I move to the couch and tentatively lift the seating. It gives. It's a sofa bed. Skeeter can sleep here. College kids aren't too fussy about sleeping arrangements.

Yeah, I could host the Clark clan, but... "Shoot, Tess, I told the real estate agent she could sublet the cabin while I was gone."

"What? Nooo!"

"Don't despair yet, I only agreed to the deal a few hours ago. I doubt she's already rented the place. Listen, I'm going into town anyway to pay my rent, I'll check with the agency right away and let you know, okay?"

After we hang up, I put on my coat and boots and hurry out of the house. I lock the door behind me and feel silly as I pause on the patio, checking the edge of the woods surrounding the cabin.

Come on, Riven, the big, bad wolf isn't coming to get you. Not today.

Still, I cross the yard at a faster pace than usual and am relieved when I make it safely to my Grand Cherokee. The old Jeep is so battered, it's the only thing Cassie won't fight to keep in the divorce—she's already taken the Mercedes.

I grab the wheel, not caring how cold it feels under my palms. This car and I, we've been on many adventures together. This ancient Jeep is the only memento of my life as it was before my soon-to-be-ex-wife hauled me into an upscale neighborhood with posher houses, posher friends, and a posher lifestyle that I hated and that never seemed to be enough for her. More, more, more. She wanted more clothes, more jewelry, more restaurants, more expensive trips...

And, thanks to California's fifty-fifty divorce laws, I guess I'll be the sucker who keeps financing her swanky lifestyle even after our marriage is over. At least until she marries another sucker.

Unexpectedly, the thought of Cassie re-marrying hits me in the guts with brutal force. I push her, the divorce, and her future imaginary husband out of my head. She's wasted enough of my life for me to keep pining after her.

As I reverse the car and turn into the snow-covered driveway, the reflection is blinding in the mid-afternoon sun. I should tell the agency to send the plowing service more often.

Until November it was manageable. But now, it snows every other day, and even when it doesn't, the wind pushes the old snow around forming snowdrifts down the road.

At least the Jeep doesn't have a problem overcoming the rough terrain. I'd like to see Cassie drive her precious Spider up here. She'd get stuck in the first mile. But I'm not thinking about my ex-wife, right?

***

The real estate agency is located in my favorite part of town, the Park City's Historic District. I love its quaint buildings and unique restaurants. And now, with fairy lights crisscrossing over the street and sparkling from every shop window, Main Street is even prettier.

I find a parking spot right in front of my favorite pub, and my stomach begs me to go in, but I prefer to sort the subletting business first. With great effort, I ignore the smell of grilled meat coming out of the pub and cross the street toward the Richter Real Estate Group's offices. I push the glass door open, prompting the wooden reindeer above the entrance to fill the room with the tingly notes of Jingle Bells.

Charlotte, a young administrative clerk, looks up from behind her computer screen and smiles. "Riven." She blushes. "I mean, Mr. Clark."

I approach her station. "Hey, Charlotte. No worries, I told you Riven is fine. How are things going?"

She pouts her lips and puffs out air. "This holiday season is pure madness. Every single house we manage is rented back-to-back throughout January. The number of check-ins and check-outs we have to deal with is insane."

She gestures at the empty office around her. "As you can see, it's all hands on deck. I have to hold the fort alone. Have you come in to drop off your monthly check?"

"Yes, that…" I hand her the check and scratch the back of my head with my other hand. "And also, Kelly Anne called me this morning…" I explain the whole sublease business and why I have to cancel.

"Oh, I'm so sorry for your father," Charlotte says when I'm finished. "What a horrible time of the year to have a burst pipe. At least in LA, all that water won't freeze overnight. Up here, it'd be a complete disaster."

"That's California for you," I say as my stomach growls.

Did she hear that?

"Hungry?" Charlotte asks.

Yep, she did.

"Yeah, sorry. I skipped lunch."

Her lips part in a bright, wholesome smile. "Let's sort your house situation, then, and you can be on your way to the pub. I won't even bother you to ask for an update on the new book."

Charlotte, I discovered, is a fan and has read all my novels. Whenever I come in, she begs me for spoilers on the story I'm working on, and I promptly refuse to give up anything. "Thank you, Charlotte, and you know you never bother me."

"Ah, you're too kind. I bet you get sick of all your fans pestering you."

"Actually, it never gets old. I love my readers."

Charlotte blushes again, and I'd better stop talking if I want her to be able to work.

"Let me just pull up the calendar." Her eyes shift from me to the computer. She clicks on the mouse a few times and frowns. "I don't see any openings in your rental. Kelly Anne must not have had time to free up the slot yet." She turns the screen toward me, showing a monthly view of December where all the days are colored in red. "I'll just add a note saying you no longer wish to sublet, and you should be fine."

She types a quick memo and looks up at me. "You're all set. Have a great lunch…" She scrunches her face in an eager but embarrassed expression. "And please finish the book soon, I can't wait to read Preacher's next adventure."

Nothing strokes a writer's feathers better than an avid reader. I smile at Charlotte and give her a mock military salute. "Will do, ma'am."

If I keep writing like today, my manuscript will be completed in no time.

Five

Riven

Three weeks later, I've written a grand total of 4020 more words—nothing! Less than 200 words per day. At this rate, it's going to take me longer than a year to finish the damned book.

I'm sitting on the living room faux-sheep rug with my back against the couch, staring at the blank page opened on my laptop, devoid of any inspiration. The text cursor blinks, mocking me in an intermittent dance that's become the bane of my existence. As if on cue, my phone rings. The caller ID informs me it's Carmen, my agent.

I'm tempted to ignore the call, but that would only postpone the conversation by a few hours, a day tops.

I tap the green button. "Carmen."

"Tell me you have something new for me to show to the editor. A page, a chapter, anything?"

Of the 4000 words I wrote, maybe 3000 are usable. "Sorry, Carmen, but I told you I'm writing this book differently. The process isn't linear. The single tidbits won't make sense until I put them all together."

Carmen remains silent for a few long heartbeats, then sighs. "Riven, you're one of my most reliable authors. Not only a sure bestseller, but an organized writer who delivers on time, which, with you artists, isn't always the case. I know you're working hard and not fooling around like some of my other fibbers who wait until a month before their manuscript is due to get down to writing…"

"But?" I prompt.

"But the past year has been stressful for you, and it's not the end of the world to miss a deadline. As long as you give us enough warning to plan ahead."

"Who's us?"

"I've spoken to the editor." Carmen sounds hesitant. "Darren Floyd has already finished his new book. The publishing house is willing to push his launch forward to next fall and postpone your release to the spring."

"But then I'd miss the holiday season. I always come out in October."

"Yes, but your first drafts are usually ready by December."

"What's Floyd's book titled?"

"*Touch of Fear.*"

I swear silently in my head, that's a damn good title. "Floyd isn't taking my spot," I say between gritted teeth. "Listen, my family is coming over this week for the holidays and I won't have much time to write. But once they're gone, I promise my butt won't leave the chair until I have something solid for you to present to the editor."

"Okay, Riv, the publishing house is giving you until the end of January. But if you don't have a first draft ready by then, they'll go ahead with *Touch of Fear.*"

"I won't let you down, Carmen, I promise."

I'm determined to use these last few hours of quiet before my family arrives—they should land mid-morning—to get down to some serious writing. But, just as my fingertips hit the keyboard, a gray Subaru pulls up in the front yard, followed by a white van with "Molly's Maids Cleaning Service" written on the side in sweeping characters.

What now? Did I forget an appointment? The cleaning agency usually comes on Fridays and today's Wednesday.

Kelly Anne from the real estate agency gets out of the Subaru and marches toward the front door in her high-heeled winter boots. She rings the bell, but by the time I reach the entrance, I hear her already using her key to unlock the door. So, when I pull it open, she jumps back, frightened.

"Oh, Mr. Clark, you gave me a scare." Then she eyes my sweatpants and cozy flannel shirt and frowns. "What are you doing still here?"

"I live here," I say.

"Yeah, okay, but weren't you supposed to leave yesterday to visit your family?"

"I'm not going, they're coming here."

Kelly Anne pales. "What? But you agreed to sublet the cabin from the 22nd to the 28th."

"Yes, but then I canceled with Charlotte and told her I'd be keeping the house for Christmas."

"When did this happen?"

"Just a few hours after you called me three weeks ago."

"Oh, my." Kelly Anne brings a hand to her forehead and collapses on the patio's log bench.

"Are you okay?"

"Yes, but I'm afraid we have a *situation* on our hands, Mr. Clark."

Kelly Anne has barely finished talking when two more cars pull up in the front yard and an assortment of people dismount, taking suitcases out of the trunks. A tall woman pulling a wheeled, gray suitcase comes up the patio front steps, smiling. She's wearing a beanie, but a few locks of blonde hair escape from underneath the hat to be trapped again under the collar of her white puffer jacket.

"Hi," she says to the real estate agent. "You must be Kelly Anne. Mindy told me you'd be our point of reference in town. I'm Wendy Nichols." Then the blonde looks at me, her light-blue gaze sending an unexpected electric zip through my body, and her smile falters. My face must not look too thrilled or welcoming. "Is—is there a problem?" she stutters, her eyes roaming from me to Kelly Anne.

Kelly Anne gets back into her everything-is-going-to-be-all-right persona and stands up to shake the blonde's hand with a bright smile stamped on her face. "Miss Nichols, very nice to meet you. And to answer your question, it appears there's been a hitch with your booking, but nothing we can't solve, I'm sure." Then she gestures at the open door. "Why don't we all get inside and see how we might deal with the situation."

"I'm not letting these people into my house," I say.

Another blonde pushes past the first one, carrying a baby in each arm, and says, "I don't know what the issue is, but I have two infants who need to get fed and I'm getting into the house, *now*." She steps in front of me, raising an eyebrow. My only option is to step aside to let her in. Which prompts all the other people in the yard to follow, workers from the van included.

Only Kelly Anne, me, and the first blonde remain on the threshold. I don't know why, but I feel as if letting this Wendy person into the house will somehow equal losing a battle.

I turn to Kelly Anne. "Can't you find them a different accommodation?"

The real estate agent struggles to keep her smile in place. "I told you the entire city is sold out."

"I'm sorry but if these people were booked in my cabin, shouldn't your team have come yesterday to get my things in storage?"

Kelly Anne nods. "They should've, but we've run into one snafu after the other. This holiday season is the craziest I've ever had, believe me. We were counting on doing it last minute today." She smiles apologetically.

"Excuse me," the blonde says. "Can someone explain to me what the problem is?"

"Miss Nichols," Kelly Anne begins. "Mr. Clark here has a long-term lease on the cabin and had initially agreed to sublet the house for Christmas week—"

"I never signed the papers," I say.

"Yes, Mr. Clark," Kelly Anne says, condescendingly. "I'm catching up on that." She turns back to Wendy. "But when he changed his mind, we must've already rented the place to you in the meantime. And my administrative team and I had some kind of misunderstanding, and they told him he was fine to stay. So, it appears we have a double-booking situation on our hands."

Wendy pouts and stares me down. "Well, since there's nine of us and only one of *him,* it seems to me it'd be much easier to find *him* alternative accommodations."

"Except the lease is in my name and I'm not about to give it up to a bunch of strangers." The blonde glares at me, but I continue, undeterred, "And even if I were willing to leave, my family is coming to stay for the holidays, and there's seven of us."

"Nine beats seven as well," Wendy replies childishly.

"Long-term lease beats no right to the house at all," I snap.

"Now, now," Kelly Ann intercedes. "No need to argue. I'm sure we can find a solution. Why don't we just walk into the house and—"

I turn to her. "What you must do is get all these strangers out of my cabin before my family arrives."

As if on cue, two more cars pull up in the front yard, which has now lost all its at-peace-with-nature vibe and resembles more a mall parking lot.

My dad and Skeeter get out of one car and Tess and her family get out of the other.

Dad is the first to walk up the front steps and immediately picks up on the tense atmosphere.

"Hi, son. What's going on?"

"Nothing, Dad. Hi."

"Nothing?" Wendy disagrees and turns to Dad, all prissy and comfortable on her high horse. "Your son wants to kick me and my family out in the snow for Christmas."

My father blinks uncomprehendingly.

"There's been a double-booking," Kelly Anne explains. "And we're trying to decide which family should get the house."

"Oh, okay." He smiles at Wendy from under his white mustache. "Don't worry, miss, no one will get kicked out in the snow under my watch—especially not at Christmas. Why don't we all go inside and try to figure out the situation in front of a hot cup of coffee?"

"That's what I've been trying to say from the start," Kelly Anne says, gesturing toward the open door. "Shall we?"

"Ladies first," my dad offers gallantly.

Wendy smiles at Dad and precedes him into the house, ignoring me completely. As she passes me, a whiff of vanilla invades my nostrils.

I do my best to ignore the pleasant scent and to glare at Miss Contempt instead, hoping she'll feel the burn of my stare on her back. But I get distracted again when she pulls off the beanie and jacket, and a cascade of white-blonde locks tumbles down her shoulders. The revelation is even more disturbing than her clear light-blue gaze. I stare mesmerized until she opens her mouth to mutter under her breath, "I guess like father, like son isn't always the case."

"What did you just say?"

She turns and fake smiles at me. "Nothing."

Once both families are assembled in the open-space living room, the situation looks even more tragic than I initially imagined. There are people everywhere.

Wendy's sister—I assume the other blonde is her sister, given the resemblance—is seated on the couch next to a man, probably her husband, each feeding a bottle of milk to a baby. Skeeter and another guy in his early twenties are perched on stools at the kitchen island.

Dad and an older woman have taken possession of the kitchen and are busy making coffee.

Tess and her husband—Noah—are standing uncertainly by the French windows. The three members of the cleaning crew are sitting on the stairs, probably waiting for instructions.

And a bunch of kids are running around the room too fast for me to count exactly how many.

And of course, there's also Goldilocks crowding my personal space with her too-sweet vanilla scent.

Next to us, Kelly Anne takes in the scene, and her thoughts must echo mine because she asks, "How many of you are there exactly?"

Six

Wendy

"We're nine in total," I answer the real estate agent. "Five adults, two kids, and two babies."

Kelly Anne looks over at Riven Clark, who until half an hour ago was one of my favorite authors on the planet, and asks, "And you?"

"Seven, five adults and two kids," he replies, in a low, deep voice that's too sexy for his own good. I peek at him sideways. Gosh, he looks even better than in the pictures on the back of his book covers. Unruly dark hair, mysterious brown eyes, full lips, and a sexy, two-day stubble. Pity he turned out to be such a horrible person. Never meet your heroes; the saying was invented for a reason.

"For a grand total of ten adults, four kids, and two babies," Kelly Anne summarizes.

"Safe to say we all agree we can't fit both families in this house," the great American novelist says.

The poor lady from the rental agency does her best to keep smiling. "Please allow me a few minutes to check what our options are with my colleagues at the agency."

She takes out her phone and moves away from the crowd. The inside of the house is scorching hot compared to the freezing temperature outside, so I remove my heavy sweater and drop it on the back of an armchair.

Riven scowls at me, saying, "Don't get too comfortable." He moves past me to go talk to the pretty brunette by the French windows. His sister? His wife? Is he married?

Why do I care?

I don't!

I join Joshua and another boy eighteen, nineteen years old tops, at the kitchen island.

"Coffee?" Riven's dad offers each of us a mug.

"Thank you, Mr. Clark," I say.

"You're very welcome, Miss?"

"Wendy, Wendy Nichols."

"What a beautiful name, and please call me Grant."

I'm halfway through my cup of coffee when the real estate agent comes back. She claps her hands, asking, "Could all the adults please join me at the dining table?"

The table is a massive, rectangular slate of solid wood—natural oak, I'd say—and it miraculously seats ten people.

Amy declines the invite and prefers to remain on the couch with the twins, which leaves Kelly Anne free to take the last spot and look us all in the eyes with a grave expression.

"I've talked to my colleagues at the agency," she intones. "I'm sorry to inform you there are no vacancies anywhere in town, nor at any of the ski resorts nearby. The only rooms we could find are at a motel off the highway in Salt Lake City."

"My family isn't spending Christmas at a highway motel," I say with finality.

"I'm truly mortified my agency put you all in this situation," Kelly Anne continues. "Especially since it'll be Christmas in three days. At the Richter Real Estate Group, we pride ourselves in providing an excellent experience for all our customers."

"We understand, Kelly Anne," Mr. Millions of Copies Sold says, surprising me with the tameness of his answer, until he adds, "I'm sure you can refund the Nicholses their fare and they can be back home in time for Christmas."

"What?" I snap. "The plane tickets, too?"

From the couch, Amy shouts, "I'm not putting the twins back on a plane today, tomorrow, or any day sooner than a week from now. And before anyone suggests it, I'm not putting them back in a car seat either, unless it's to go somewhere super close. They're done traveling for the day. Right, little munchie-pies?" She coos at them, and then, back to her normal voice, she adds, "So you people had better figure something out."

"Well, someone has to go," Riven says. "And it won't be my family." He purses his lips in a stubborn, bratty—although sexy—pout.

"Actually..." Kelly Anne wrings her fingers, "... what if we could find a solution to host everyone here?"

"What?" Riven sputters. "Are you seriously proposing to cram sixteen people into a house that barely fits half that number?"

"We can try," the agent insists. "You still wouldn't have to pay April's rent, Mr. Clark. And your family, Miss Nichols, would get a full refund of course."

"That all sounds very nice," Riven says. "But it's just not possible."

"Son." Grant puts a hand on Riven's shoulder. "It's Christmas. Do you really want to send these people on the street to spend the holidays in a cheap motel?"

"I don't *want* to, Dad. But I don't see what the alternative is. We can't all fit in the cabin."

Mr. Clark senior—my new personal hero—smiles benevolently from under his crispy mustache. "I believe this gracious lady"—he gestures toward Kelly Anne—"was telling us she could do some creative bed-shuffling if we let her."

Kelly Anne jumps at the opportunity and nods. "Thank you, Mr. Clark." From her messenger bag, she takes out a large A3 blueprint of a building and places the sheet of paper on the table with the blank side facing up. "Let's make a headcount first. Wendy, could you please tell me again your names?"

On the right-hand side of the sheet, she writes a list starting with my name. "There's you?"

"My sister, Amy, her husband, Trevor."

Kelly Anne writes their names underneath mine.

"The twins," I continue. "Her two younger kids, my mom—"

"Emily," my mom interrupts. "Nice to meet you all."

"And my brother, Joshua," I conclude.

Kelly Anne writes the last name and stares up at Riven expectantly. "And on your side?" she asks, already writing his name down.

"There's me, my father Grant, my sister Tess, and her husband, Noah, her two kids, and my brother Skeeter."

"All right." Kelly Anne stares at the list and draws four square boxes next to it, saying, "We have one master bedroom, two singles, and the small room with the bunk bed." She adds another box. "Then there's the sofa bed that can sleep two."

"That's five beds for fourteen people," Riven points out sourly.

"Patience, Mr. Clark," Kelly Anne says. "We could put Amy and Trevor in the master bedroom with the twins. I already have the traveling cribs in my car."

"Fine by me," Amy yells from the couch while Trevor nods in front of me.

"All my stuff is in that room," Riven protests.

"We can help you move everything," Kelly Anne replies, nonplussed, while pragmatically crossing four names off the list. "Now, Grant and Emily, I thought you could both get one of the single bedrooms. One has a twin bed and one a full."

"The lady can have the full bed," Grant says with a jovial smile.

And is my mom blushing as she thanks him in response?

Kelly Anne writes Grant and Emily in the boxes representing the single rooms and, with two efficient slashes of the pen, removes them from the column of people awaiting sorting. She looks up and studies my brother and Riven's brother who have their heads bent together as they stare at something on their phones—probably some secret, young-people app the rest of us have never heard about.

"You two," the real estate agent addresses them directly. "Would you have a problem sharing the sofa bed?"

Joshua and—I spy the name from the column—*Skeeter* look at each other and shrug.

"Cool by me," Joshua says.

"Yeah, dope, man."

They bump fists while Kelly Anne strikes out two more names and sighs. "Now the tricky part."

Riven sulks. "You mean the part where four adults and four kids share a bunk bed?"

Kelly Anne bites the end of her pen, thinking, then turns toward the crew of maids still sitting on the stairs. "Molly, can you please have a look at the attic and tell me if there's any way we can turn it into an extra bedroom?"

"Come on, girls," the oldest woman stands up. "Let's go check what's up there."

The maids disappear up the stairs and Kelly Anne goes back to staring at her "house map."

"The kids," she says. "We're never going to find beds for them." And while Riven scoffs and crosses his arms over his chest in a satisfied told-you-so attitude, Kelly Anne adds, "We'll need to get creative… The basement is small but cozy and, most importantly, dry and warm. What if we had the kids sleep on the carpet on cots or sleeping bags… we could even make it an indoor camping experience, I could have a few teepees brought in. What do you say?" She addresses the question at Riven's sister.

But before she can answer, one of the Clark kids, a girl not older than eight with dark, straight hair, pulls on her mother's sweater, pleading, "Mom, I want to do the indoor camping. Can we? Pretty please?"

Riven's sister bends and kisses the girl on top of her head. "Sure, honey."

"And, Mom?"

"Yes?"

"When are we eating? I'm getting hungry."

Grant stands up and looks at my mom. "Emily, since we two old foxes are already settled, what do you say we make lunch for the whole crew? See what my son has stashed in the fridge that we can work with."

"What a wonderful idea." My mom stands up, smiling in a way I haven't seen her smile since Dad passed.

From across the room, I shoot a look at Amy to check if she's noticing something as well. My sister raises an eyebrow at me and shrugs, meaning: I saw, but I'm as clueless as you as what to make of it.

In the meantime, the crew of maids comes back, and the leader delivers her report. "The space upstairs is good. Ample enough to fit a double bed and a small closet. But it hasn't been cleaned in a while, it's going to be a hard job. It'll take my crew all day to finish and I'll have to call in a second crew to do the rest."

Kelly Anne smiles brightly. "Thank you, Molly. Please call in the reinforcements and I'll have the movers come with the furniture tonight."

Molly nods. "I'll start right away."

Kelly Anne thanks her again and goes back to her paper, her pen striking six lines on the list in quick succession while she mutters, "The kids go in the basement... and Tess and Noah take the attic."

Only my name and Riven's remain in the columns. He stares at the list, probably thinking the same thing, and his frown deepens as he does the math a heartbeat faster than me.

My mouth is already gaping in horror when Kelly Anne unleashes her most dazzling, killer smile on us and asks, "Riven, Wendy, would you mind sharing the bunk bed?"

Seven

Riven

All eyes turn on me, and I don't see how it's fair since the question is technically addressed to two people. Guess everyone assumes I'm going to be the *difficult* one.

Shaking my head, resigned, I say, "I'm okay with that if I can take the lower bed." When I was eight, I fell off the top bed once and I've done my best to avoid bunk beds ever since. I guess after twenty-five years of success, my luck has run out.

All eyes now turn to the other half of this arrangement.

Wendy blinks at me. "I don't mind staying on top," she says with total innocence.

Pity, a vivid image of what she'd look like *staying on top* in a very different situation invades my mind, making my eyes widen. I'm not quick enough to hide the shock, and Wendy catches me. She frowns at my reaction, then her eyes narrow.

Thankfully, Kelly Anne chooses this moment to resume talking with all her artificial cheerfulness. "Then everything's set." With clear satisfaction, she crosses my and Wendy's names off the list, writing them in the last box in her drawing.

"Sorry to interrupt." My dad places his hand on my shoulder. "Riven, did you get any groceries?"

I turn to him. "No, Dad, I was waiting for Tess to get here because I never know what's considered edible these days, like if we're doing Paleo, or Keto, or whatever diet Tess is trying out this time."

From across the table, my sister shows me her tongue and then rolls her eyes to the rest of the people, raising a single finger. "One time I tried to be pescatarian, and he's never going to let me forget it."

"Not when you made me eat moxarella cheese," I shoot back and, turning to the others, I add, "It tastes nothing like real mozzarella."

My dad pats my shoulder. "Well, then I'm afraid there's no way we can cook for fourteen people."

"Actually," Kelly Anne stands up, "what if I booked you all into a nice restaurant in town while I and the crew take care of everything back here? Afterward, you can visit the ice arena, and by the time you come back tonight, the house will be ready. Sound good?"

Getting everyone ready and into the cars is no simple task. My head already aches at the mess the next week is going to be. If I could hope to sneak a few writing hours here and there while my family was visiting, with this horde invasion, it'll be impossible.

I bring my computer along to lunch anyway, hoping maybe I'll be able to sneak off to a café later when everyone will go to the ice arena. At the restaurant, the two families break down the middle and each faction claims one half of the table. I sit at the farthest end where there'll be no chance of me having to talk to one of the Nicholses, not even to pass the salt.

That's how I end up spending two hours being brought up to speed on grade school gossip by my niece and nephew. Once the bill is paid, I try to quietly slip away, but Tess catches me and kindly informs me all family activities are mandatory this week. And Dad insists that I should bond with our new friends.

Resigned, I follow them to the arena, put ice skates on, and glide along the rink like a good boy. When our hour is up, the women decide we should hold another assembly to draft a shared grocery list. The kids go for another round while the adults sit on the bleachers to confer. My head threatens to explode as I listen to everyone's food quirks—kids and infants included since apparently, the twins have a favorite, irreplaceable formula. Then the list gets split into five sub-lists and Tess, Dad, Wendy, Wendy's mom, and I are each assigned a section of the supermarket to make the grocery shopping more efficient. We take a car while the remaining parents allow the kids yet another round of ice skating.

By the time we get home, the maids' van is gone, and only Kelly Anne's Subaru is parked out front. The men unload the groceries while the mothers wrestle the kids out of the cars. At the main door, with this many people, an actual line forms. I swear it's the first time I've ever had to queue to get into my house. The process is particularly long since during our earlier assembly it has also been established that shoes should be removed before walking inside.

When I finally get in, Kelly Anne is greeting everyone with that ever-present annoying smile of hers. She has a kind word for every new person coming in: "Welcome back. Did you have fun skating? What do you think of the old town? Was lunch good?" … and so on.

From over my grocery bag, I peek at the house and I have to admit I've never seen it in such good shape. It looks like a brand-new home where the movers have just removed the protective film from the new furniture, not a speckle of dust to see anywhere.

"Kids." Kelly Anne claps her hands. "Would you like a tour of your new camping grounds?"

Shouts of approval fill the room and the kids run toward the basement stairs, losing hats, gloves, and scarves along the way. Tess and Noah follow them, collecting both their and the other kids' stuff. They keep what's theirs and hand the rest to Wendy's sister and her husband, who are each holding a baby in their arms and couldn't easily pick up stuff from the floor.

"Thanks," Amy says to Tess. "Shall we go check out the camp as well?"

Besides the fact that they've invaded my house, the Nicholses seem to be nice people. And everyone pretty much gets along. I throw a sideways glance at the kitchen, where Wendy is stuffing the fridge with the fresh groceries. She catches me looking and frowns. Well, with one glaring exception.

The kids are ecstatic about the indoor camping and ask if they can stay in the basement until dinner is ready. We ordered pizza since it's too late to cook a meal for fourteen, and the moms agree to let the children play until the delivery arrives.

I step in line and wait for my turn to get a peek at the basement. When I do, I have to give it to Kelly Anne: she did a great job. The washer and dryer have been moved to the far corner and camouflaged behind a curtain with a forest painted on it. Four small tepees occupy the rest of the space and are each equipped with a sleeping bag, a flashlight, and a steel water bottle engraved with the real estate agency logo. There's also an assortment of pillows scattered everywhere.

On the adult front, Tess and Noah can't stop gushing about how beautiful their attic bedroom is. Kelly Anne takes in all the positive feedback and her smile loses the forced quality it has kept all day.

She approaches me. "Mr. Clark, my apologies again for the misunderstanding."

I don't have it in me to keep a grudge. "It was an honest mistake," I say. "Could've happened to anyone."

Her features relax further. "Thanks so much for understanding. I know you came here to write in peace and this"—she points at the room full of people—"must be less than ideal. But it's only for a short week. Oh, and before I forget, we've stacked most of your things in your father's room. There wasn't enough space in the small one. Same for Miss Nichols, she's sharing a closet with her mom."

I nod just as the doorbell rings.

"That must be the pizzas," I say.

"And my cue to go." Kelly Anne grabs her coat from the back of the couch. She claps her hands to get the room's attention. "Good night, everyone, I'm leaving. Please don't hesitate to contact me if you need anything at all. And merry Christmas."

A choir of goodbyes and merry Christmases follows as I usher Kelly Anne to the door where two skimpy delivery guys are waiting on the porch, each holding a tower of seven pizza cartons.

"Mmm, smells heavenly," Kelly Anne comments as she wiggles out between them. "Bon appétit, Mr. Clark."

"Skeeter!" I shout for my brother to come give me a hand. He and Joshua arrive and each takes a stack of pizzas while I pay.

There's isn't enough space at the big table for the kids, so they eat sitting on the rug in front of the couch, using the coffee table as their dining base.

The pizza is from my favorite Italian restaurant in town and delicious as always. It does wonders to lift my mood. My family and "the other family" also seem in a pretty good mood. Especially my dad. I'd even go as far as saying he's doing his best to impress and entertain Wendy's mom.

"Riven," Wendy's sister calls halfway through dinner. "Can I call you Riven?"

"Sure, Amy," I say. From the list Kelly Anne used to sort the rooms, I've applied mental name tags to all the Nicholses. "How can I be of assistance?"

The twins have been put to bed, and for once both Amy and her husband have two free hands. Amy cuts a slice of pizza, but before bringing it to her mouth, she gives a sassy grin. "Now that you've stopped frowning for a minute, I was wondering if you wouldn't mind telling us what your next book is going to be about? I'm a huge fan."

The conversation at the table dies while all heads swing my way.

I scratch the back of my head. "So, you recognized me?"

Amy swallows the mouthful of pizza. "Hard not to, when your books are in the front windows in every bookstore around the country—airports, too." She turns to her husband. "Trevor, didn't you buy one of his novels to read on the plane?" Then back to me. "I told him I already had it in eBook, but he prefers paper."

"Which book?" I ask.

"*The Black Veil.*" Trevor nods. "It's amazing. Actually," he hesitates, "would you mind signing it for me?"

"I'd be happy to."

Trevor stands up. "I'll go grab it."

45

"If you wake up the twins, you're dead!" Amy shouts after him. She strikes me as a very direct person. Or maybe, being a mother of four, she has zero time to waste on niceties.

From the other end of the table, the other Nichols sister rolls her eyes.

"Why the face, Wendy? Not a fan of my work?" I call her out.

"No, it's not that. I was just wondering how your large ego was going to fit in the bunk bed." She sidesteps the question.

Trevor comes back and hands me the book. "I'm dying to know what happens next."

A bookmark divides the paperback about in half. I smile. "Oh, you're in for a few more twists."

"I can't wait. I'm probably going to lose sleep reading it. And I'm a father of twins, so sleep isn't a commodity I have to spare."

I'm distracted from the compliments by Wendy standing up and collecting the pizza boxes. "Is the recycle bin outside?" she asks.

"Yes, at the back of the house."

"I'm taking this out."

"Don't!" I yell, standing up abruptly.

Wendy freezes in place, raising an eyebrow at me.

"I forgot to tell you all something." I snap my fingers in the couch's direction. "Kids, come here, you need to hear this, too."

The children already look sleepy after the long day of travel and an afternoon spent skating.

They each climb on a parent. My nephew, on Tess, and his sister, on Noah. Similarly, the Nichols boy goes to sit on Trevor and the girl on Amy.

When I have everyone's attention, I say, "No one should go out at night on their own, especially not the youngest. A lone wolf is prowling the woods around Park City. The town marshal believes it's an old wolf shunned by his pack. The old male is desperate, hungry, and dangerous."

"Mom," Wendy's niece, who must be five or six, cries out. "I'm scared." She hides her face in Amy's neck and begins to sob quietly.

Wendy glares at me. "You make children cry for fun?"

"I'm serious," I insist. "There've already been two attacks. The county has a ten-thousand-dollar bounty on the beast."

The girl's crying worsens.

"Would you stop?" Wendy says.

"Better scared than eaten," I say.

The wails reach ear-splitting volume and are soon joined by those of the twins upstairs.

"At least I've finished eating," Amy sighs. "And it was time for their feeding, anyway." She stands up with the crying girl in her arms. "Mom, can you take Vicky?"

Emily nods.

Amy drops the girl in her grandma's lap and kneels next to them. "No one is getting eaten, sweetheart," she comforts her daughter. "What that nice gentleman was trying to say is that we're safe inside the house, but for no reason should you or your brother go outside without an adult. The yard isn't fenced in like the one at home, and it's not safe, okay?"

Vicky rubs the tears from her eyes and nods.

Amy kisses her cheek and ruffles her blonde bangs before standing up. "Brave girl." Then she rushes to take care of the twins.

Still glowering at me, Wendy shakes the boxes already in her hands. "Should I drop these in the kitchen and wait until tomorrow to take them out?"

"I can take them," I say.

"Why?" she asks. "You taste too grumpy even for the big, bad wolf?"

We negotiate to bring the cartons out together. And after a trip to the garbage bin where no one gets eaten, we help tidy the table and kitchen.

When everyone else drifts to their rooms, Joshua and Skeeter set up the sofa bed, leaving me fresh out of excuses to postpone hitting the sack.

I stare at the lone door to the downstairs bedroom, then at Wendy...

Bedtime, I guess.

Eight

Riven

"You can use the room to get changed," I say. "I'll go upstairs."

Wendy nods, looking as weary as I feel. "Thank you."

I wait for Skeeter to be done in the upstairs bathroom and change in there. I take my time trying to avoid the unavoidable until I have to accept my destiny and return downstairs. Wendy is already in bed with a laptop on her legs, typing. The room is filled with her vanilla scent, and I can only say I'm glad she's wearing a sensible flannel pajama. As un-sexy as pajamas go.

"Good night," I say, getting in the lower bunk.

The bed is too small. If I try to lie flat on it, my feet poke out at the other end. I experimentally curl on one side in a fetal position, not exactly comfortable but... Gosh, I miss the California King upstairs.

I close my eyes and try to relax.

Click-clack-click-clack-click-clack.

The sound of Wendy's typing drills a hole into my head. I turn to the other side, pull the covers up to my ears, push the pillow over my head... nothing works. The persistent click-clacking from above prevents me from sleeping.

Exasperated, I get the pillow back under my neck and ask, "Is the typing going to last for long?"

"I write better at night," Wendy replies, nonplussed.

"Of course, Goldilocks," I say. "Besides stealing people's beds and writing at night, do you East Coast gals also smoke Marlboro Lights and drink Cosmopolitans a la Carrie

49

Bradshaw?"

"No," she replies curtly.

"What are you writing anyway, a sex column?"

The noise stops and she sighs, exasperated. "I'm working on my new play, and if you don't mind, I'd like to get the scene down while it's fresh in my mind."

I grab my phone from the tiny nightstand and covertly google 'Wendy Nichols plays' while saying, "I can't sleep if you type, and tomorrow we have to get up very early." Both families agreed to hit the slopes at first light.

Her legs swing over the top bed, and I drop the phone to my chest to cover the screen, once again thankful for the flannel PJs and wool socks covering every inch of her skin. Wendy hops down from the bed, skipping the tiny ladder, and rummages in her night bag, retrieving a small packet.

"Here." She hands it to me, bending over. Her face too close. "They gave me earplugs on the plane, they're new. I didn't use them."

Without waiting for a reply, Wendy heaves herself back to the top bed and the click-clacking resumes, relentless.

I sulk in silence, not sure if I'm more resentful she's writing, or that she *has* something to write—contrary to me.

Before putting the plugs in, I check the search results on my phone. Every single one is about a recent Broadway musical she wrote: *Forgotten Dreams*. The name sounds familiar. I remember reading a gushing review about it in the *New York Times* a few weeks ago—even if I live on the West Coast I subscribe to the *NYT*, both to read reviews of my novels and to keep up to date with the bestseller charts.

'Electrifying, riveting,' the article said about the play. The praise was so unusual from the normally severe theater critics that it stuck with me.

Mmm. Goldilocks is a fellow writer. I wonder how she got into plays, why she doesn't write novels, and, especially, what story she's working on right now so intensely. There's nothing worse for an author with writer's block than being stuck with someone who's hardly able to get away from their keyboard.

I put the phone back on the nightstand, checking once again that the alarm is set for five thirty, and insert the plugs in my ears. The noise magically disappears.

I curl under the covers, shooting one last mental curse upstairs, *let's see how happy you'll be tomorrow to have written all night.*

***

When the alarm goes off the next morning, Wendy groans as if in actual physical pain.

"What time is it?" she mumbles.

"Five thirty," I reply tersely, retrieving my laptop from under the bed.

"Why did you set the alarm so early? We don't have to leave for another two hours."

"I write better in the morning," I say, opening the manuscript to the last chapter.

"Argh," she growls. "That's *so* West Coast. Do you also start the day with a celery smoothie?"

"No, just coffee like everybody else. You want to go make a pot?"

She surprises me by saying, "Sure, right away." Wendy hops off the bed and shuffles out of the room.

She comes back fifteen minutes later with two steaming mugs of coffee and offers me one. "A chalice of writers' poison for you, sir."

I take the mug and sniff it suspiciously. "Did you put *actual* poison in it?"

Wendy smiles angelically. "No poison, I promise." She winks and climbs back up on her high tower.

The coffee smells fine, with no suspicious scents. I take another heavenly sniff and bring the mug to my lips for a long sip. But as soon as the dark liquid reaches my tongue, I sputter it back out, narrowly avoiding dropping the whole mug into my lap.

She put *salt* in my coffee. Loads of salt.

"Something wrong?" she thrills.

I get out from under the bed, dropping the mug on the windowsill and dabbing at the spatters on my T-shirt.

"You put salt in my coffee," I accuse.

"Really?" Wendy asks, keeping up the angelic facade. "Sorry, I must've confused the jars."

I narrow my eyes at her mug. "Does your coffee have the same seasoning?"

She smirks and half hides her mouth behind the mug. "I drink it black."

Instinctively, I know she's lying. "Give me your mug," I say.

Wendy doesn't protest and hands it over. The liquid inside is a few shades shy of *black,* closer to a golden caramel color. I take a sip. Damn, she puts vanilla even in her coffee, and it's the best thing I've ever tasted.

"You've converted me to black coffee," I say and raise the mug in a mock toast. "I'll keep this."

Wendy shakes her head, amused, and gets off the bed and out of the room, presumably to make herself another cup.

I finish the coffee and get back into my tiny bed. Using a corner of the bedsheets, I dry the computer screen from the spatters of salted coffee, which won't become a thing—like salted caramel—and power up the laptop.

Once again, I come face to face with my worst enemy: the blank page.

By the time Wendy comes back, I haven't written a single word. As she hops on the top bed, the pressure to perform increases.

Preacher pulled Wyatt on the stone ledge next to him...

I write and stop. Where are they going? How will they find a hospital for Wyatt in the middle of the Ethiopian mountains?

"That's ten words tops you wrote," Wendy calls from above after a while. "Did you wake me up to write ten words?"

I count the words: *exactly* ten. Talk about turning the knife in the wound.

"I'm stuck, okay?" I confess.

Her face drops level with mine, but upside-down. "Take a break, then."

"I can't. I've written close to nothing in the past month and I'm on a deadline."

Wendy sighs and retreats above. "Gosh, I hate you. I'm bone-tired, but I can't go back to sleep. Are you having plot issues? Character issues? Why are you stuck?"

"I don't know."

"Are you writing another Preacher Jackson story?" she asks.

I sit up straighter as she admits knowledge of my work. Has she read my books? Did she like them? I don't ask any of those questions and just answer, "Yes."

"Where is he this time?"

"Ethiopia."

"Doing what?"

I haven't shared details of my upcoming novel with anyone but my agent and my editor, but with Wendy, I feel safe to divulge. Maybe because she isn't asking as a fan, but with a clinical approach. "Retrieving the lost Crown of Twelve Stars worn by the Woman of the Apocalypse."

"Okay. Does he have the crown already?"

"Yes."

"That's half the book. Why are you stuck, again?"

"Preacher and Wyatt just got out of a cave and are trapped on a ledge at the edge of a cliff. But Wyatt is wounded so they can't 'mountain climb' their way out, and I don't know how they're going to find a hospital in the middle of the forest?"

"Mmm." Wendy thinks for a second. "Do they *have* to come out on the edge of a cliff? It seems like you're writing yourself into a corner on purpose. Couldn't they just exit the cave in the forest and stumble into a missionary camp where Wyatt can be cured?"

I frown. "That seems too easy. Where's the adventure in that?"

"Then put a few more obstacles along the way. Make them fight with a panther or something."

"Preacher already fought one in the cave."

"Okay, then make them retrace their steps until they find a fork in the tunnels. Oh," Wendy says excitedly, and the bed shakes as if she jumped up sitting. "They could find the panther's lair and discover she was a mother and has left a cub behind. The kitten is too small to survive on its own, so Preacher and Wyatt take it along…"

"A pet panther?" I ask skeptically, while still writing a list of bullet points.

- Escape into the forest
- Missionary camp
- Pet baby panther?

"Yeah, you know? Or just google 'dangers Ethiopian jungle' and see what comes up."

I do as she says and add a few more bullets to the list:

- drug traffickers
- thieves
- poisonous animals
- antigovernment guerrillas
- smugglers' route
- quicksand

"Find anything interesting?" Wendy asks after a while.

I stare at the notes, pleased. "Yep, I should have enough leg-work for a few more chapters." I shut the laptop and get out of bed, bracing against the top bunk guardrail. "You're almost forgiven for the salty coffee."

Wendy rolls her eyes, smiling. "How magnanimous of you."

I clap my hands. "But now it's time to get up for real. What do you say we get breakfast started for everyone?"

Nine

Wendy

Okay, I expected Riven would react a lot worse to the coffee prank. But the man has shown he knows how to take a joke in style. He's not a total grump.

Why is the thought more disconcerting than reassuring?

Because if he was just a pompous, grouchy windbag, it'd be easier to ignore how good-looking he is, or how genius his writing is...

"...What do you say we get breakfast started for everyone?" he asks me now, offering me a hand to get off the top bed while flashing that front-cover smile of his—the smug grin of someone who can make you happy in bed and knows it.

Alarm bells jingle all over my head, and I summon my inner censor. *Wendy Nichols, should I remind you you're already spoken for?*

No, I tell my conscience, while noticing Brandon hasn't even texted me to ask how the journey went or if we arrived safely.

I take Riven's offered hand and push off the bed, but I misjudge the impetus of the jump and land squarely into his arms, almost knocking him over. Riven somehow manages to steady himself and keeps both of us upright.

His body is warm, his eyes brown and inviting like a cup of hot chocolate, and his full lips are the color of strawberries. I bet they even taste sweet.

Oh my gosh, I'm such a creeper.

"Sorry." I clumsily get off him and basically run out of the room.

In the kitchen, we brew more coffee to add to the pot I'd already made. With ten adults, a single pot isn't going to cut it. Then we lay the table and try to remember whatever foods the various members of our families are having for breakfast.

Joshua and Riven's brother keep sleeping on the couch, unperturbed by all the noise we're making. They don't even stir when my phone rings.

Ah, Brandon must finally be calling.

No. It's Mindy.

"Hey," I pick up, taking mugs out of the cabinet with my free hand.

"Hi," she says. "Sorry I didn't call sooner to check on you, but I had a crazy day yesterday."

"No problem."

"How's the cabin? Is everything all right?"

I hesitate. "The house is fantastic, really."

"You don't sound convinced."

No point in hiding the truth from my best friend. The double-booking wasn't her screw-up after all, but I know how much Mindy cares about her job. She won't like it. But even if I kept quiet, she'd find out when the refund receipt of the holiday landed in her inbox. So I might as well rip the Band-Aid. "No, no, the house is gorgeous…"

"But?"

"But there's been a double-booking mishap?"

"A what?" Mindy shouts. "You're sharing with someone else? How could that happen? I'm going to call the Park City agency right away."

"No, no, please. We've already sorted everything. The real estate agent is giving us a full refund, and we have somewhere to sleep that isn't a motel on the interstate, so we're cool."

"But how did it happen?"

Holding the phone between my shoulder and my ear, I open the fridge and take out the various kinds of milk—non-fat, 2%, almond, and soy—spreading the cartons at regular intervals along the table. "A guy is renting the cabin long-term, and he said he was going home for the holidays, but then his family came here instead—"

"His *family?* How many people are there in the house?"

"Sixteen."

"How are you managing that with four bedrooms?"

I get the phone back in my hand and move behind the counter to pick oranges for the juicer. "The kids have tents in the basement, and the agency put an extra bedroom in the attic."

"Where are you sleeping?"

"I'm sharing the bunk bed with the guy."

"Is this *guy* hot, by any chance?"

Riven drops his elbows on the counter next to me, saying, "Please don't hold back your praises on my account."

I almost drop all the oranges I've picked up.

Mindy has one of those piercing voices clearly audible over the phone even by someone standing ten feet away. I didn't expect the conversation to take this turn and didn't think of lowering the speaker volume.

"Was that him?" she asks.

"Yes, it was, and you might be able to judge the graciousness of his looks by yourself... he's Riven Clark."

"Riven, who? Wait a moment, you can't mean *the* Riven Clark. Multiple number one *New York Times* bestseller?"

I sigh. "Yep, him."

"Oh my gosh. Does he look as hot as on his covers in person?"

"Mindy, he can hear you, and you're puffing up his already inflated ego."

Riven flashes me his signature smug grin.

Undeterred, Mindy continues to embarrass me. "Please tell me I can call Brandon and dump him on your behalf so you can go have a roll in the snow with the hot writer."

I throw a side glance at Riven and notice his smile has lost some megawatts.

"No, you can't dump Brandon on my behalf," I hiss, lowering the speaker volume and moving to a corner of the room where Riven can't hear us.

Ten

Riven

Of course she has a boyfriend, man, how stupid can you get?

How was I supposed to know? Wendy came without a plus one and no ring on her finger... It was easy for me to assume she was single.

Better this way.

Fewer complications.

Now I only have to endure her sweet vanilla scent for a few more nights, ignore her blue-eyed gaze and blonde tresses, and pretend she's not a woman who'd talk plot points with me all night long.

One night down, six more to go.

Easy peasy.

Wendy hangs up with her friend and comes back to the kitchen sporting an awkward smile.

"That was Mindy, my best friend. Sorry, she knows no boundaries."

"It's okay, I have a best friend who's much the same." *Don't ask her about the boyfriend. Don't ask her about the boyfriend.* "So, you have a boyfriend back in New York?"

"Yeah, Brandon," she says. *What a douchy name.* And then, even if I haven't asked, she adds, "He couldn't come because of work. He's trying to make partner at his firm."

"Lawyer?"

"Investment banker."

Ouch, even worse.

"What about you?" Wendy asks, her cheeks flushing. "Dating someone?"

I'm saved from the misery of answering by the sudden influx of family members. One moment we're alone—if you don't count our sleeping brothers—and the next, the room is full of people. They shuffle down the stairs, sporting various degrees of lingering drowsiness, guided by the smell of fresh coffee like a small army of zombies to the ring of a bell.

Breakfast is noisy and chaotic, but I honestly don't mind it. After seven months of hermitage, I didn't realize how much I missed having people around.

Once everyone's belly is full, Wendy and I are excused from doing the dishes since we've already made the meal, and we're granted dibs on the two upstairs showers. She uses the master bathroom in "my" room now occupied by her sister and the twins, and I'm in the common bathroom. While I'm showering, I have to fight hard to chase off a mental image of Wendy being presently naked in my shower. Guess the vision will haunt me long after the Nicholses are back in New York.

Man, it's been too long since you've been with a woman if you're fantasizing about someone who'd pour salt in your coffee not even twenty-four hours after meeting you.

True. I can't even remember the last time Cassie and I had sex, and that was long before she filed for divorce seven months ago, so…

When I get back to my temporary room, Wendy is zipping up her ski suit—all-white, belted at the waist, and with an array of pockets scattered all over. With her blonde hair cascading down her shoulders, she looks like an angel. Then she tilts her head slightly backward and pulls her hair up in a high ponytail, which is even sexier.

Too sexy.

Instead of stating any of the compliments shuffling through my head, I goad her, "That suit new? It's not going to stay white long."

She pulls on the ponytail to tighten it, looking me straight in the eyes. "The suit is new, but I'm not worried about it getting dirty."

"It will the first time you fall."

Wendy walks up to me on the way out of the bedroom and pauses a second to stare me down, "I don't know about you, Clark, but *I* don't fall."

Ooooh, so Goldilocks thinks she's got game.

Challenge accepted.

The trip to the slopes is short, but getting everyone ski-ready is not as easy. I'm the only one who doesn't have to rent skis, poles, and boots. So, while the others go to the rental shop, I buy day passes for the whole crew. Since the two families are about the same in number, Tess has set us up with this expense-sharing app where we all log in what we've paid for—groceries, ski passes, restaurants, etc.—and the app automatically calculates at the end of the vacation who is owed what by whom.

Who is owed what by whom, if I wrote a sentence like that in one of my books, my editor would bring out her alliteration whip and flay me.

Ski passes bought, equipment rented, with the kids in ski school, and the twins dropped off at a slope-side childcare facility, the adults are finally ready to go.

I sit on a bench to strap my left boot to the board and, paddling with the other foot, I join the others getting in line for the chairlift.

When I pass Wendy, she eyes me sideways, saying, "Of course you'd snowboard."

"Something against boards?"

She just shakes her head, whispering under her breath, "West Coast."

"Think you can beat me on those, East Coast?" I point at her skis.

"You'd be lucky to catch my trail."

We bicker all the way to the turnstiles and just as we're getting in line to board the carriers, I take advantage of Wendy fumbling with the elastic of her ski pass to claim the last spot on the incoming one.

"Hey," Wendy calls after me, "I was next!"

The chair arrives and cuts my legs from behind in a gentle motion, forcing me and the three other passengers to sit. Once we have the bar down and are secured in place, I turn back to wave at Wendy. "See you at the top."

"So," my sister says next to me as we begin the upward journey 75 feet off the ground. I'm sharing with her, Noah, and Dad on the other side. "You seem to have *bonded* with the pretty blonde?"

Karma.

I should've let Wendy go first. My punishment is to spend the next fifteen minutes fending off questions about my personal life that either I don't want to answer or don't have the answers to. The interrogation culminates with the question everyone I know has been pestering me with since I left LA.

"When are you coming home?"

"When I've finished the book." I give Tess the standard reply.

Partially because if I keep going at this snail's pace, I'll never finish the damn thing. And secondly, because I'm not sure *where* home is. The house I used to share with Cassie and probably won't recognize once the works are completed? That's not home. It hasn't been for a long time.

Thankfully, the chairlift reaches the mountain top, and I'm spared from more callous questions.

I shake off the wistful mood as I slide around the chairlift station in the warm morning sun. I stop at the edge of the slope to fasten my other boot in place and admire the view.

From up here, the mountains are breathtaking. I take a deep inhale of air so crisp and clean, like it no longer exists in cities, and examine the terrain. A snow squall has passed through last night, leaving a clear, cloudless sky and four inches of perfect skiers' snow. It's early enough that the ground is still freshly groomed in an almost intact corduroy. These are the best snowboarding conditions: great visibility, predictable control, and no ice. Almost as good as fresh powder.

I've little time to admire the scenery, though, because as soon as the next lift arrives, Wendy pushes on her poles around the flat arrival area and, without a moment's hesitation, launches past me and down the slope, yelling, "Last one to arrive is a loser!"

I pull on my goggles and dive past the edge, enjoying the immediate adrenaline rush of speed and cold air.

Wendy wasn't kidding, she's good.

To keep in her wake, I have to push forward, holding nothing back. She stays in the lead for the entire race.

But toward the end, the decline becomes more gradual, making it the perfect bunny slope for beginners where a bunch of inexperienced skiers is moving down in ample turns, snowplow style. One veers unpredictability and cuts Wendy off, forcing her to swerve violently at the last second and to come to an abrupt stop. I skim right past her, waving, and cut through an imaginary finish line.

Wendy follows suit and scrapes to a halt next to me, sending a jet-spray of powdery snow over my board.

Before I can gloat, she cuts me off, "This one doesn't count. I would've won if not for that idiot who blocked me."

"Hazards of the competition, Nichols. Come on, don't be a sore looooooser," I mock her, using my fingers to make an L shape on my forehead.

Wendy scrunches her face, frowning while trying to suppress a smile. "I want a rematch," she says, pushing ahead, ready to embark on the chairlift another time.

She gets more than one rematch.

In fact, we end up racing each other all day long. Sometimes I win, sometimes she does. By the time the resort closes, I've lost count. But even if the drill is exhausting, I'm sad when it gets dark and we have to go back to the house.

In the car, Tess brings her hand over my forehead as if to feel my temperature.

"What are you doing?" I ask.

"Checking if you're okay."

"Why?"

Tess winks at me. "Because you can't stop smiling."

Eleven

Wendy

Every muscle in my body hurts as I climb the ladder to the top bed at not even nine o'clock in the evening. By the time we got back from the slopes, it was past five and it took a few more hours for everyone to change and shower.

I went last so that I could enjoy every drop of hot water without having to worry about preserving it for the next in line. I filled the tub in Amy's en suite and soaked in scorching water until every single one of my muscles was mellowed. After the long bath, I changed directly into my pajamas and sank into the closed-for-daytime sofa bed, refusing to get up for any reason—including having dinner.

Almost everyone followed my example.

Today, skiing conditions were so perfect that no one wanted to stop and we ended up eating lunch super late at a slope-side restaurant at three in the afternoon. And not a light meal either. Fatty foods are supposedly the best to keep warm.

Only the kids and the college-attending duo, still blessed with faster metabolisms, fought over the pizza leftovers from last night. The "real" adults—even if Joshua and Skeeter technically classify as adults, I don't include them in the category—were fine nibbling from a tray of fruit Riven's sister had peeled and sliced.

The only energetic person in the gang was Amy, who swears skiing all day is resting, compared to having to take care of the twins.

Riven follows me into the room two minutes after I've scooted under the covers. He takes one look at my exhausted self and, leaning against the bed, smiles.

Even in the short time we've spent together, I've learned that Riven's smiles have a lethal combination of charisma and primal sex appeal. The way the right corner of his mouth draws up, the perfect curve of his upper lip, the fullness of the lower one, and that sparkle in his eyes: intelligent, teasing, irresistible.

Steady, Wendy, steady.

You have a boyfriend back home and you're only here for a week.

Right, I'd better remember that.

"No midnight writing, Goldilocks?" Riven asks.

"No," I confirm, too exhausted even to fight with him. At the moment, I have to make a conscious effort to keep my lids open. And I suspect I'm succeeding only because Riven has hypnotized me with his crinkly brown-eyed gaze. "You? Please tell me you won't set the alarm for five thirty to write another ten words," I tease.

"Only if you promise not to spike my coffee with salt ever again."

I nod.

He knocks on the wooden guardrail. "Good night, Goldilocks."

"Night."

Riven disappears below deck. And without his spellbinding stare on me, nothing prevents me from closing my eyes and falling asleep on the spot.

***

The next morning, I blink awake as a bright ray of sunlight pierces my closed lids. I turn my face away from the light and pull the covers up to my chin, listening in the silence for any sign that Riven is still asleep underneath me.

But no tell-tale sound of regular breathing or faint snoring reaches my ears, so I dare to lean my head overboard and peek. The lower bunk is empty.

A worrying pang of disappointment twists my stomach. I wanted to see how he looked while he slept.

I grab my phone and shoot a quick text to Mindy.

> Is it a bad thing if I want to watch Riven sleep?

> No, it's freaking awesome

> Please tell me you also want to see his sex face

> Dump Brandon, go have fun

I should've known I'd get this kind of response from Mindy.

> I won't dump Brandon to have a one-night stand

> Not after I invested almost two years in the relationship

68

And a relationship shouldn't be something you invest in

Do you even love Brandon?

What kind of question is that?

The only kind you should ask yourself when deciding if you should be with someone for two years

I can't do this before coffee

Have coffee

Shave your legs

Bang the hot writer

I shake my head and drop the phone under my pillow as if to hide Mindy's words. I hop off the bed and pull a robe on, moving into the kitchen.

Riven is already behind the counter making coffee. Amy is up, too, warming a bottle of milk.

"Good morning," I say.

Amy huffs. "Ah, easy for you to say you're having a good morning when you're childless," she rants. "This is the second bottle I've had to make because Rob already regurgitated the first while I was feeding him, *in bed.* The sheets are a mess. I had to call the agency and ask for replacements. I hope the puke didn't soak into the mattress or we're never going to get rid of the stink."

I throw a side-glance at Riven since that's technically *his* room—*his* mattress. Amy must realize the same thing because she touches his arm, saying, "I'm sorry, you probably came up here to write without distractions and we're disrupting your retreat."

Riven smiles. And not even a fake or perfunctory, polite smile that wouldn't reach his eyes. No, it's with real warmth that he says, "No problem, who cares about the mattress… Is your son okay?"

"Oh, yeah, yeah, don't worry, it's perfectly normal for infants to vomit, he just swallowed his milk too fast."

The bottle warmer beeps and Amy retrieves the milk to then disappear up the stairs.

I replace my sister at the counter and pull mugs out of the cabinet. "Amy didn't plan on twins," I say. "Well, I guess no one ever plans on twins, but hers are the random case."

"There's a *not* random case?"

"Yeah. The non-identical ones happen when two different eggs are fertilized at the same time, and they run in families. Sometimes they skip a generation, but they can be kind of expected. Identical twins come out when an egg splits in two for whatever reason, and they're totally random."

Riven pours coffee in the mugs I've prepared and sets up another pot for refills. "You the expert on twins?"

"When Amy found out she was having twins, it's all she could talk about for months, so, yeah, she made us all experts of sorts."

In a seamless rhythm, we finish making breakfast and setting the table just as our families come strolling into the living room. No one agreed to a precise alarm time like yesterday, but everyone still got up at the same hour as if we've all transformed into one massive, living organism.

Once everybody has had coffee and something to eat, Tess clears her throat. "How do you guys want to get organized for tomorrow? Should we just compare family recipes and decide what goes?"

She's talking about the Christmas meal. I hadn't thought another family may have different traditions. But they're from California. What if they only eat enchiladas for Christmas? Or this could turn into that episode of *Friends* where everyone wants a different kind of mashed potatoes. Oh my gosh, what if they do apple pie instead of pumpkin pecan?

Mom surprises me by saying. "If I may, Grant and I talked about this last night and thought that we, as heads of the families, could take care of the meal. We'd only need someone to drive us into town today for the groceries."

"I can do that, Mrs. Nichols," Riven offers.

"Thank you, and please call me Emily."

"Mom, it's okay," I say. "Amy and I can help with the cooking if you don't want to."

Mom blushes. "Oh, don't be silly, dear. Who else would cook if not me?"

I shoot a stare at Amy, wanting to say: *didn't we come here specifically because she was too old to cook for eight people, and now she wants to cook for sixteen?*

Amy shrugs in a don't-know-what-to-tell-you way.

Riven's niece pulls on Tess's sleeve, asking, "Mom, what are we doing today? I'm too sore to ski again."

Tess ruffles her daughter's hair. "Like everyone else, honey."

"I have a list of cool things to do Mindy gave me," I say, reaching into the pocket of my robe for my phone and then remembering I left it on the bed. "Phone's in my room, I'll go grab it."

I stand up and cross the living room to the door of our bedroom. When I enter and reach for the phone under my pillow, the screen lights up with a bunch of notifications from Mindy.

> Counter-order

> DO NOT bang the hot writer

> I repeat: DO NOT bang the hot writer

> I did some research

> He's married!

I stare at the words without comprehending their meaning. Or rather, I know what "married" means, but he can't... Riven can't...

That doesn't make any sense

I type back.

How can he be married?

From the way he talks, he's been up here alone for a while

At least I'm pretty sure he doesn't. I would've noticed a wedding band if he had one on his finger.

Mindy's reply comes in an angry tweet.

He could've taken it off the moment he saw you

He wasn't exactly expecting me

And where would his wife be?

How could she not be here for Christmas?

How could Brandon not be there for Christmas?

He had to work, you know

Maybe his wife is a scumbag who works all the time as well

But for months?

I don't know

But read this

It was at the end of one of his books

Mindy sends me a picture. It's a shot of a print book page titled Acknowledgments.

I suppose I should start with my parents, to whom this book is dedicated and whose love for reading inspired my own. Thank you for reading to me every night when I was growing up, for never telling me I was too old for fairy tales, and for empowering me to follow my dreams.

None of this would have been possible without my fearless and lovely agent, blah, blah, blah.

Over the writing of this novel, I've had the honor of working with several fantastic editors. To Fiona Harper: thank you for taking a chance on this book, and for your insightful and genius editorial guidance throughout the years. I am a better writer for having worked with you.

He lists a series of other names. I scroll the page faster, skipping all of them.

To the entire team at Rumpelstiltskin Press, who have worked so tirelessly on this book.

Another list of useless names.

To the team at the Carmen Rhodes Literary Agency:

More names. I skim through them all until I reach the next paragraph, and my heart stops.

To Cassie, my wife: What can I say? I've known you for almost as long as I've been working on this book—and what a journey it's been. Every day, I wake up with joy and gratitude in my heart because

The page cuts here. I quickly text Mindy.

> **Send me the rest**

Another pic arrives at once.

I get to walk this road with you. Thank you for taking such good care of me, for being my best friend, for making me laugh, and for carrying me when I felt like I couldn't go on. I wouldn't have made it without you, and I'm so excited and blessed to go on this next leg of the journey with you.

Reading these words leaves me breathing hard. Wow, I mean, I know he's a talented writer, but what it must be like for a woman to receive such a dedication. I fire another quick text to Mindy:

> **What book was this from?**

> *The North Star*

I check on Goodreads. *The North Star* is his debut novel. I open the reading app on my phone and search my library for Riven Clark. I've read seven of his books. In turn, I check each title, scrolling to the acknowledgments page. Each contains a different version of the same dedication:

To my wife, Cassie: You are my light, my rock, my best friend, my safe harbor—basically, my everything. Thanks for loving me, for joining me on this incredible journey. Your laugh is my favorite sound in the entire world.

To my wife, Cassie: Every day with you is a gift and a joy. I'm so lucky to have such a loving, fun, and spectacular friend to go on adventures with around the world. Here's to many, many more.

They're all the same. My best friend, my soul mate, my adventure buddy... He sounds so in love. This is a couple I'd tag #RelationshipGoals on Instagram. They wouldn't spend Christmas apart.

I check the Goodreads list again. I've bought all of his books except for the latest release that came out this past October. Once more, I switch apps and buy it in a few quick clicks. I tap my foot and bite on a fingernail as I wait for the book to download in the app and then immediately scroll the table of contents to find the Acknowledgments link.

The page loads up and, with a beating heart, I do a forensic scan of his declarations of gratitude. To my readers, to my editors, to my family, to my agent... No wife.

I take a screenshot and send it to Mindy.

> This is from his latest book

> Maybe they're separated?

> You'd better make damn sure before you do anything

> I don't want to do anything

> I'm just curious

Mindy's only reply is a Pinocchio emoji.

Twelve

Wendy

"Mind if I call dibs on the shower?" Riven asks, making me jump.

I turn around, hiding the phone behind my back as if I were concealing a dirty little secret. My eyes immediately dart to his left hand—definitely no ring.

Riven frowns. "Are you all right?"

"Yes, sure, why wouldn't I be all right?"

"So, is it okay if I use the shower first?"

"Yeah, yeah, no problem." I shuffle past him and out of the bedroom.

In the open-space living room, almost everyone has scattered. I sit back at the table where my plate is still waiting with a half-eaten slice of toast on top. Tentatively, I take a bite, but it's gone cold and chewy. I drop it on the plate again and clear the table. I need another cup of coffee.

As I pour coffee into the filter, I consider what the best option would be to investigate Riven's past. I could ask his sister, but Tess would probably read too much into my sudden interest. Any woman would. What about his father? Even if Grant is a guy, he seems like the insightful kind. And if his son is going through a divorce, he could be protective about it. How about Skeeter? If Riven's brother is anything like mine, he's still in that chill-dude phase where he doesn't overthink, and guys always give more straightforward answers.

But how to ask? I can't just approach him and say, *hi, we've never spoken before, but is your brother still married by any chance?*

As if summoned by magic telepathic waves, Skeeter materializes next to me and asks, "Is there any extra coffee?" He stretches his arms over his head. "The couch is killing my back. I spent half the night trying to find a comfortable position."

"Sure," I say, and then add, "I'm so sorry we barged in on your family holiday."

Skeeter shrugs. "Wouldn't have made much of a difference, I was supposed to sleep on the couch, anyway."

"I hope you don't mind sharing with Joshua."

"Nah, your brother's cool. But we're considering getting sleeping bags and joining the kids in the basement. I mean, the floor can't be worse than that couch."

"Oh, I bet the kids would love to have their cool uncles join the camp."

"Yeah, we might hop into town and ask Kelly Anne for sleeping bags, maybe even an air mattress. How about you? Is my brother a cool roommate?"

"When he doesn't set the alarm at five o'clock to write, yeah." This gives me the perfect opening to pry. "Does Riven always go on a retreat when he has a book to finish?"

"Nope." Skeeter grabs two clean mugs for me to fill. I pour the coffee and he takes one, adding, "But he had to leave LA after his dirtbag wife left him for a soap opera dude with their house halfway into a remodel."

Chill-dudes, always to be relied upon to provide answers.

"Oh, I'm so sorry," I say, even if I'm not sure that "sorry" is an accurate description of how I feel. Is it bad that I'm relieved Riven's wife had an affair and left him?

So bad.

"Yeah, it hasn't been the best year for my brother."

Skeeter finishes his coffee in one long sip and, acting as if we hadn't just finished discussing his brother's crumbling life, he says, "See you later."

"Later," I say. My phone is in my hands before Skeeter has circled the kitchen island.

> The wife left him for a soap opera actor

Which actor? Which soap?

> I don't know

Who told you?

> His brother

Okay

You're in the clear

Are you going to bang him?

"Hey." Riven's voice makes me jump.

I look up from the phone screen to find him standing next to me, barefoot. That must be why I didn't hear him approach. He's wearing jeans and a flannel shirt. His hair is still wet, and he's drying it with a towel draped around his neck.

He smells like a sunny mountain day: fresh snow, pinecones, cold air, and hot kisses.

Wendy, get a grip, no one smells like hot kisses.

But if someone could, Riven would be that person.

I look into his crinkly brown eyes, searching for any sign of heartbreak. What must it have been like to have the woman he loved, his wife, his best friend betray him in the most horrible way?

"Hey, you," I reply.

"Shower's free if you want, and I know you were looking for cool activities to do"—he jerks his chin toward my phone—"but everyone has decided they want to go into town and buy a Christmas tree for the house and decorations." Riven flashes me one of his high-voltage smiles. "I've been scolded for not providing one."

Why didn't you? I wonder silently. *Is it something you used to do with your wife?*

"Oh, that's a wonderful idea. I love decorating the Christmas tree."

"Yeah, I didn't bother this year because I figured it'd be a waste since the family was only going to be here for a week, and I'd have to throw everything out afterward. But Kelly Anne assured us there are plenty of charities we can donate the decorations to for next year."

"That's fantastic! Picking ornaments is my favorite part."

"You should hurry, then. They want to leave in half an hour."

They.

My smile falters. "You're not coming?"

"Nah, I thought I'd take advantage of the quiet house to write."

Now I want to stay, too, but of course, I can't. Unless I want to start acting like a pathetic groupie.

I raise my mug in a mock toast. "I'll leave you to your baby panthers then."

"I can't promise I'll put the baby panther in, but if I do, I'm dedicating my next book to you, Goldilocks. For curing my writer's block."

Riven winks at me, and my stomach responds with a somersault.

"It'd be an honor," I say, and leave before he notices how big of a smile he's put on my face.

The idea of replacing Cassie in his special dedication fills me with a ridiculous amount of joy.

This is silly. I have a boyfriend. And even if I didn't, I'm here only for another four days and then I'm back in New York. And whenever Riven finds his footing again, he'll be back in LA.

Two worlds apart.

***

Still, as I get dressed in the bathroom after a quick shower, I'm unable to wipe the smile from my face. What will he write about me? It won't be something as strong as what he wrote about Cassie. I'm not his best friend, we're not in love, and I'm most definitely not his wife.

Will it be a short line like: *To my fierce bunk-bed mate and our sleepless mornings spent discussing plot points?*

Umm, nah, I don't know. It was *one* morning. And does he see me as fierce? How does he see me? Probably like a crazy person, I did salt his coffee less than twenty-four hours after meeting him. In my defense, he'd tried to kick my family to the curb at Christmas and unnecessarily woke me up pre-dawn, so.

To my holiday roommate, thank you for the plot points and the salt in the coffee?

I need to stop obsessing about this. The promise of a dedication is probably something he said without really meaning it. By the time he's finished the book, he probably won't even remember me.

My stomach drops with unease at the thought. I find the idea of him forgetting me sad. Why couldn't he live on the East Coast? It is a truth universally known that the tormented writer stereotype fits better in New York.

Wendy Nichols, even if he lived in New York, you'd still have a boyfriend.

Right.

A boyfriend who still hasn't called or texted me once since I got here. I pick up my phone and dial Brandon's personal number—screw office hours.

"Hello..."

"Hi, Bra—"

"Hello? ... hello? ... Just Kidding, leave me a message."

Gosh, I hate his voicemail message. It gets me every single time; no matter that I must've listened to it a million times.

The line beeps and I hang up. Better to send him a text than leave a message he'll never listen to. But he precedes me with a single-line text:

> At work, babe, talk tomorrow

The message is so frustrating, I don't bother to reply. I doubt Brandon will even notice. Disappointed, I yank on a fluffy cream wool sweater and pull on cream corduroy pants, ready to cheer up with a little Christmas shopping. When I get out of the bathroom, everyone who's going into town is already busy pulling on their coats.

"Wait for me!" I yell at the mass of people, and hurry toward my bedroom to pick up a pair of beige suede Timberland boots from my suitcase—they're perfect for this outfit.

I rush into the bedroom and collide with Riven coming out. He grabs me by the shoulders and steadies me on my feet, saying, "Careful, Nichols."

Then his eyes widen as he takes in my outfit. I look down at my chest, checking the fabric for stains or I don't know, a tear, perhaps?

"Is something wrong with my sweater?"

Riven stops staring and meets my eyes. "You like white, uh? It suits you," he adds with a curt nod before sidestepping me to go into the living room.

Blushing, I follow him with my gaze as he sits at the dinner table, facing the window, and, laptop in front of him, begins to write. He's wearing one of his button-down knit sweaters that gives him a hot nerd vibe. He puts on a pair of black-rimmed glasses and the look is complete.

"Wendy!" Amy yells. "Are you coming?"

"Yeah!" I shout, and open my suitcase to find the boots while trying really hard not to make a mental inventory of all the white clothes I brought.

Thirteen

Riven

I swear if she pulls another white sweater out of that suitcase, I'm going to throw it all into the fire. Now that the house is finally empty, I'm sitting at the big table, supposedly writing. But instead of staying with Preacher and Wyatt as they crawl out of the cave and into the jungle, my mind keeps drifting back to Wendy and how beautiful, huggable, soft, warm, and sexy she looked this morning dressed again in all white.

My phone buzzes on the table, and for once, I welcome the distraction, especially since it's my best friend calling.

"Hell—"

"Have you had sex yet?" Danny cuts me off before I can finish saying hello.

I take back everything I just thought, I'm not glad he's calling. Not in the least. Danny has been pestering me for months to "enjoy" my newly single status when I can't find anything desirable about my new situation.

"No," I say. "No sex, not any soon."

Am I, for the first time since the divorce announcement, regretful in saying this?

"I don't understand why you aren't getting laid, dude."

"And I told you a million times, I'm not ready."

"Buddy, I'm not talking about commitment or a relationship. I'm talking about putting yourself out there. Jump back on the horse…"

"Danny, drop it, I'm not getting on Tinder."

"I still don't see why you should be so resistant to dating apps, but if you want to be old-fashioned about it, you're in the perfect setting to meet women."

"A cabin in the woods?"

"A mountain resort where tourists come and go, eager to have fun for a weekend. It's the perfect situation: you find a nice lady, enjoy her company for a few nights, and then she's back on a plane headed home. No risk of getting attached, no heartbreak, only good times."

I fit the phone between my cheek and shoulder and get up to make myself another pot of coffee. "Well, your love rehabilitation program will have to wait at least until next week."

"Why?"

"I already have my hands full with tourists at the moment."

"Meaning?"

While I make coffee, I explain the double-booking situation and my current sleeping arrangements.

"Is this Wendy gal hot?" Danny asks once he's up to date.

"I suppose so," I say noncommittally.

"Oh my gosh, you like her."

"I don't *like* her," I say. "She's crazy. She put salt in my coffee the first morning she was here."

"Why?"

"Because I woke her at five to write and because I tried to send her family away to sleep in a cheap motel for the holidays."

"Ow, feisty. This is good news, bro, great news, actually!"

"No, it's not. And even if I liked her, which I don't, it wouldn't matter. She has a boyfriend."

"So? It's still good news to me."

"No, it isn't, you know how I feel about cheating…"

"Dude, I'm not saying to sleep with a spoken-for woman. But we should celebrate all the same."

"Why?"

"Because it means your Bangaloo is alive."

"My Bangaloo? What's a Bangaloo?"

"Your junk, your male reproductive organ. It has finally come out of hibernation, resuscitated from the dead. Now the road's wide open for you to meet new women. The first one is always the hardest."

"I'd rather not discuss my private parts as if talking about a person."

"Let's not discuss them at all then, let's put them to use. Now that I think about it, you probably need a wingman or you're never getting out of that cabin. I can't come until after the end of the year, but I'm going to check my calendar for January and see if I have a few free days to come visit."

"Danny, the last thing I need is another distraction. I have to work on my novel."

"Trust me, sexual release will be the best writing booster. Of course you can't write, dude, not with all that pent-up sexual frustration. I'll look at my dates and let you know. Now I've got to go, man, but I'll text you when I book my flight."

I shake my head as Danny hangs up, no point trying to explain personal boundaries to my best friend. And to be honest, now that I'm getting used to having people around again, I'm not sure how I'll feel next week when they'll all be gone. When *she*'ll be gone.

You'll be free to write in the morning or at night, whenever you want.

Right, which is what I should be doing right now. I finish my mug of coffee, pour another one, and get back to work.

Preacher stumbled forward, carrying Wyatt with him. His friend was a dead weight now. Preacher had to pull on the arm Wyatt had slung over his shoulders to keep him upright while his other arm, wrapped around Wyatt's waist, bore most of his friend's 200 pounds. They couldn't keep going like this for much longer.

Something stirred in Preacher's backpack, and he cursed himself for the millionth time since he'd decided to save the cub. He needed to be carrying the extra weight of a baby panther like he needed an elbow shoved up his—

A scream tore through his mental cursing. He looked up and his knees buckled with relief. A cluster of nuns with dark skin were fleeing at the sight of him, running toward a nearby encampment. A mission.

They were saved.

Among the chaos, a vision appeared to him, an angel. Tall, blonde, with alabaster skin, and eyes the color of the sky. The woman came to the edge of the camp to check what all the fuss was about. She was wearing khakis—

No, not khakis.

White, she should wear all white. Yes, white scrubs, she's a doctor. I delete the last paragraph and re-write it.

Among the chaos, a white woman hurried out of a tent. Tall, blonde, with eyes the color of the sky, she was dressed in white head to toe—white scrubs, a doctor's uniform. For a moment Preacher thought he was hallucinating, that he was having a vision of an angel descended from heaven to take them with her. Until the woman's eyebrows drew closer together and her eyes narrowed, "Who are you?" she asked, her tone not exactly welcoming.

"Preacher Jackson." Even with the extreme strain talking caused him, he took a shot at gallantry. "At your service."

The doctor stared him down, unimpressed. "You can't stay. The militia leaves this camp alone because I keep neutral. The deal is I teach the village's children and tend to the sick, but I steer clear of the conflict."

"My friend *is* sick, he's wounded."

"And past puberty by a few years, he's no innocent." Her gaze was steady as it met his. "I'm sorry, I can't help you. I can't risk the lives of all the nuns and children living here. If I help you, I'd be putting everyone else in danger."

Preacher summoned the last reserves of strength he had to argue with the stubborn woman. "You took an oath. If you turn us away, my friend will die."

She glared at him with angry blue eyes. "One night," she said. "I'll patch up your friend as best as I can, and then you're on your own."

Preacher tipped his hat at her. "One night is all we need, ma'am."

"It's Willow," the woman said and then shouted something in the native tongue.

Two burly nuns appeared out of a tent carrying a stretcher.

The three women hurried to relieve him of Wyatt's weight, and Preacher was finally free to collapse onto his knees. Unfortunately, the move gave Willow an unobstructed view of the contents of his backpack.

Her eyes widened and her jaw dropped. "What's that in your backpack?"

"Panther cub," he said, removing the backpack from his shoulders. "You wouldn't happen to have some spare goat milk, would you?"

I re-read the page and crack my knuckles, satisfied. Carmen always begged me for a romantic subplot in my stories. And while I never saw Preacher as the fall-for-a-random-gal kind of guy, I'm suddenly inspired.

Fourteen

Wendy

In town, we divide and conquer. Joshua and Skeeter go to the real estate agency to ask for sleeping bags. Mom and Grant head to the grocery store. We leave the men—Tess's and Amy's husbands—in charge of picking an evergreen tree and securing it to the top of one of the cars, while Amy, Tess, and I stroll around the shops with the kids in tow, hunting for Christmas ornaments and decorations. We scour the one-of-a-kind stores for the prettiest shiny balls, porcelain angels, elves, and hangable snow globes.

After lunch, we stumble upon an ornament-crafting workshop and I'm not sure who's more excited about attending, the adults or the kids. By the end of the afternoon, we've produced a respectable array of cotton-stuffed felt ornaments: white snowmen, red Santas, yellow bells, and brown reindeer. Tess even crafted the cutest sled for the reindeer to pull, sewn with green yarn around the edges and embellished with glitter. Our handmade projects add the right amount of warmth to the fancy store-bought ornaments and complement them to perfection.

Back at the cabin, unpacking and hanging everything around seems like another Christmas feast before Christmas. The atmosphere couldn't be more cheery if we tried. The smell of Mom and Grant's cooking fills the house. Amy has put a classic Christmas songs playlist over the speaker system. And the decorations highlight everything with a sparkle of bright colors.

The last step is to hang a wreath on the front door, a simple evergreen circle with a red velvet bow. Tess and I use an over-the-door hanger so as not to damage the wooden door with a nail. We position and reposition the bar to make sure the wreath is hanging exactly in the middle of the door and, once we're satisfied, we exchange a proud nod.

Gosh, the house looks amazing. The tall tree sparkles with fairy lights in a corner, stockings hang from the fireplace, and mistletoe dangles from the ceiling...

Fifteen

Riven

When the troops return home, I help carry inside the mounds of food, decorations, and the giant Christmas tree.

Once the tree is up, my niece corners me to explain in excruciating detail all the ornaments she made. By the end of the account, I'm such an expert in felt manipulation I could open a handmade store.

But I have to admit the house looks ten times warmer now that all the ornaments are up and with the Christmas tree sparkling in a corner. Throughout the decoration process, I spy on Wendy. I take in the childlike joy on her face as she hangs the balls on the tree, admire her bright smile as she sprays faux snow on the mantle, and hangs the stockings with her nephew. And I shake my head as she and Tess spend a good half hour engineering the perfect hanging solution for a door wreath, making sure the circle of evergreen twigs dangles exactly in the center of the door. The process also lets in a draft of cold air that chills the house in no time.

Time to build a fire. Burning logs will be the final touch to the perfect Christmas atmosphere. I go out the kitchen back door and carry in chopped timbers from the outdoor firewood rack.

"Uncle Riven," my nephew stops me on my second round. "Can I help you with the wood?"

I turn back to answer him without looking where I'm going and promptly bump into Wendy, her vanilla scent invading my personal space.

"Sorry," I mutter.

Before Wendy can reply, her niece screams. "Auntie! You're standing under the mistletoe with Mr. Riven, you have to kiss him now."

Wendy and I stare up at the treacherous plant and its red berries, and then our gazes meet...

Sixteen

Wendy

I swallow hard as I stare at Riven, petrified. He's standing in front of me, his arms horizontal and full of logs.

"Kiss, kiss, kiss," the children chant around us.

Riven smiles teasingly. "Hey, it was your idea to decorate the house."

I frown at him.

His smile falters slightly. "We don't have to kiss if you don't want to."

I shrug as if I didn't care. "It's bad luck not to. Theater people are very superstitious."

Since he can't exactly grab me with his hands full of logs, I take a step closer to him and rise on tiptoes to give him a peck on the lips. The wood in his arms ensures enough space remains between us for things not to get too personal. But the moment my lips touch his, even if for just a second, they get seared. Heat spreads from my mouth to my face and neck and ears and shoulders. A burning current that makes me wonder what a real kiss from Riven would do to me.

I pull back immediately, as if after an electric shock. Riven stares at me, as mesmerized as I feel. I look away, too confused to think, speak, *breathe.*

The kids cheer and applaud around us, and I use the acclamation as an excuse to act as if the whole business meant nothing. I curtsy to them like the best ballerinas I've seen on stage and clap along, pretending I'm unscathed.

Once the spectacle is over, the kids disperse, searching for their next adventure.

I do my best to avoid meeting Riven's gaze again, but I covertly track him out of the corner of my eye as he proceeds to the fireplace. When his back is turned to me, I watch as he kneels down and constructs a sort of pyramid with the logs. His nubuck leather boots are unlaced, his flannel shirt unbuttoned, and his jeans tight as sin on his muscular thighs… good thing his ass is covered by the shirt. Now I get why mountain men romance is a thing. I never got a lumberjack fantasy before, but now I find myself wondering how soft the sheepskin in front of the fire is and if it'd keep me warm if I happened to be lying on top of it naked…

Which is my clue to stop ogling Riven and escape to the upstairs bathroom for a cold shower. I lock myself in, but before stepping into the shower, I send a quick text to Mindy:

> I stepped under the mistletoe by mistake and had to kiss the hot writer

Once I finish typing, I step into the shower without giving Mindy time to reply. I turn the faucet to the max hot temperature—because no one ever really took a cold shower voluntarily—and relax both my mind and my muscles under the hot jets.

When I come back out, my phone is brimming with notifications.

> I'm impressed, Nichols

Getting the mistletoe to do your dirty work

How was it?

Hey, you can't tell me you kissed the hot writer and then disappear off the face of the earth!

Are you there?

I type a quick reply.

I'm here

I was in the shower

Gimme details

Quick

To use a cliche: brief but intense

I'm having fantasies about sheepskin-in-front-of-the-fireplace sex now

Good! Dump Brandon and go live your fantasies

For the hundredth time, I'm not dumping Brandon

And I couldn't live my fantasies even if I were single

There's like a million people in the house

You could move the sheepskin to your room

Not as nice as next-to-the-fireplace sex, but... a close second?

> I'm not throwing my life in New York out the window for four nights of fun

> Correction. You'd be fixing everything that's wrong with your life in New York

> And get four nights of passionate sex as a bonus

A knock comes on the door.

"Yes?" I say.

"Wendy, is that you in there? It's Tess... are you going to be much longer? There's kind of a line out here; everyone wants to shower again before dinner."

"I'll be out in a sec."

I gather my things, shooting Mindy a quick goodbye-talk-later text. Her reply is almost instantaneous:

> Less talk, more action!

Still wearing only a bathrobe, I exit the bathroom.

"Sorry," I tell Tess on the other side of the door.

"Oh," she takes in the bundle of clothes in my arms. "You could've changed inside."

"No worries, I came up sort of on an impulse and forgot my clean clothes downstairs. It's no problem, I'll go get changed in my room."

I tiptoe down the stairs, holding the bathrobe tightly around my body while still carrying my dirty clothes with me. I stop on the last step checking that the coast is clear. My room is a few steps away from the landing, so I only have to make sure the people in the living room are distracted to stealthily run the few paces to the door. Then I'm in.

I try to lock the door, but there's no lock. Probably because it's a room intended for kids. Shoot. I'll just have to be quick.

I drop my dirty clothes on my bed and without removing the bathrobe, I pull up a pair of clean panties. Then I wrap a clean bra around my waist to hook it on my belly. Once the tiny clasps are fastened, I turn it around and pull it up to cover my boobs. But to pull the straps over my shoulders, I have to drop the bathrobe.

Of course, that's the instant Riven comes into the room. He gives a shocked cough and mutters a frantic, "Sorry."

I barely have time to peek behind me and catch sight of his widened gaze before he's run back out of the room again.

I shrug.

It could've been worse.

I could've been naked.

Seventeen

Riven

White cotton panties shouldn't, by any standard, be sexy. Unless a certain lady I'm forced to share a bedroom with decides to flash them at me. The image is going to haunt me forever.

What was she even doing getting changed in our room? Wasn't it an implied rule we should use the bathroom to undress? Did she do it on purpose?

No, I don't think so. But between that stupid mistletoe kiss and now this…

Is there a memory-erasing app? These days, there's an app for everything. There should also be one to forget how soft her lips were pressed on mine, the tingle that shot down my spine as we kissed, and the image of Wendy half naked looking at me over her shoulder.

"What are you thinking about?" Tess drops her elbows on the table next to me, making me realize I've been sitting, staring at blank space for who knows how long.

"Uh… err… plot points." I give her my standard response for when I don't want to reveal what's on my mind.

"Preacher must find himself in a tough spot, you look tortured."

Ah, I mentally scoff. Right now, I'd probably feel more relaxed if a commando of mercenaries were after me. I'm seriously considering going out for a cooling walk—big, bad wolf or not.

"Yeah," I say to Tess. "Same as usual."

"Is the book progressing?"

To my surprise, my answer is a definitive, "Yes."

Weird how I got more written today, in the few hours I scraped off family "fun," than in the last month of total peace and solitude.

"Are you coming home soon then?" Tess is notorious for her tendency to never, *ever* relent.

"I'm coming home when I'm coming home," I say and get up. "I should probably go check on the fire."

***

I manage to avoid both my sister and Wendy for the rest of the evening, but come bedtime, there's no escaping the shared-bedroom situation.

I'm last in line to use the bathroom, so when I get into the bedroom, Wendy is already there clad in her cute flannel PJs rummaging in her suitcase.

Flannel PJs aren't cute! A voice rages in my head. *They're the anti-sex.*

Well, not on Wendy Nichols.

"Hey," I say.

"Hi," Wendy replies looking up at me.

And since I don't want this to be any more awkward than it needs to be, I add, "Sorry about earlier, I didn't mean to barge in on you like that."

Wendy stands up, and this room really is too small. We're barely a foot apart. "Nah, don't worry, it was my fault. I went to take a shower and forgot to bring a change of clothes. And this door doesn't have a lock, so I thought I'd just make a quick job of getting dressed and—"

"Of course, I walked in on you."

She smiles. "Yep."

"Maybe we should establish a code. Hang a sock on the door if you're naked."

At the word naked, she blushes slightly—and could she get any cuter?

"Sock on the door if I go nude again, got it!"

The moment she says *nude,* I engage in a battle of will not to picture her totally naked.

And lose sorely.

My brain is currently photoshopping the mental image I have on file of her in her underwear, obliterating the white cotton parts and substituting them with flawless, smooth skin.

"Riven, are you okay?"

I blink. "Yeah, sure, fine."

"You kind of spaced out on me for a minute."

Yeah, I was busy fantasizing about your body.

I don't say anything.

Wendy half smiles, half grimaces awkwardly. "Well, good night."

She climbs onto her bed, and I do the same in mine. I lie down, staring at the wooden planks under Wendy's mattress. I want to talk to her, but I don't know what to say. In the middle of my indecision, Wendy's phone begins to vibrate on the windowsill.

She hangs half out of the bed to retrieve it and whispers, "Hello."

"Babe," a male voice replies.

Ah, this must be the infamous boyfriend.

"Hi, Brandon," Wendy says still in hushed tones. "Is everything okay? Isn't it super late in New York?"

"Yeah, sorry, I just got home from the office and I was pouring myself a drink at home and I couldn't help but think about you in that Agent Provocateur set I bought you for your birthday."

Oh, perfect. Now *I* can't help but picture her in racy lingerie. And given the effect cotton underwear had on me, I'm pretty sure even the simplest Agent Provocateur set would fry my brain for good. I mean, the whole brand was invented to tease, it's in the name!

"Now's not the moment," she replies in an even lower tone.

"Come on, babe, I miss you." The guy's voice is barely audible now. Wendy must've lowered the phone's volume. But in the night's quiet, I can still make out his words as he says, "Play with me."

Hooray.

The dude wants to have phone sex.

I point a finger gun to my temple and shoot an imaginary trigger.

"Brandon, are you drunk?" Wendy hisses.

"I had a few drinks after work; I'm not drunk. I'm horny, and I want to—"

"Stop. You don't call me in days, and the first call I get is a drunken phone-sex booty call?"

"Hey, relax… what's the matter with you?"

What's the matter with you, dude? I've never seen the guy, but I feel an irrepressible urge to punch him in the face.

"Listen, I have to go now." Wendy sounds irritated. "Talk tomorrow?"

"Well, your loss. Merry Christmas to you, too, I guess," the guy replies, and then must hang up because the room goes quiet.

The silence lingers for a long time until Wendy whispers, "Please tell me you're asleep and didn't hear a word of that."

She must be talking to *me!*

What do I do? What do I say?

For lack of a better alternative, I let out a theatrical snore, then another, and another, until Wendy begins to laugh.

She chuckles for a while and then in a tone between serious and mortified, she asks, "So you heard?"

And while I didn't particularly appreciate her boyfriend's crassness, I don't think Wendy needs to hear me say as much. "Come on," I joke. "Can you blame the guy? He must miss you."

Wendy sighs. "I don't know. Tonight is the first time he's called since I got here, and it wasn't to ask me how I was or to have a conversation. He was drunk and horny and not at the office for once. And it's like he remembered, oh, yeah,"—for whatever reason, she says the next part in a drooling southern lilt—"I could call that girlfriend of mine and have myself a little phone sex."

A bout of laughter escapes my lips. "Sorry," I say.

"You're laughing at my misery?"

"No, it's just that I really like your narrative style. If you get bored with writing musicals, give romantic comedies a shot."

"Yeah, sure, only I wouldn't know how to write a happy ending for this one."

The conversation is taking a dangerous turn, but I try to keep my replies objective. Same as I used to do when I discussed problems of the heart with Tess in high school and college before she met Noah. "If he doesn't make you happy, nothing forces you to stay with him."

"I can't bear to add another failed relationship to my tally, and I don't want the last two years of my life to have been a waste."

"So instead, you plan on wasting even more time on the wrong someone. Great thinking, Nichols."

"You sound like Mindy now."

"Is that a good thing?"

"If you take pride in being a fiercely independent woman, sure..." She pauses for a second and then adds, "Thank you..."

My eyebrows rise. "For what?"

"For not being a dick about the phone call."

"What can I say? I have a soft spot for women who invade my home and spike my coffee with salt."

Wendy stays quiet for a long time. So long that I assume she's fallen asleep. But then she whispers, "You're not the worst roommate either. Night."

"Night," I reply, suppressing a heavy sigh.

I've already survived three nights. What's four more...

Eighteen

Wendy

On Christmas Day, we spend the morning outside, making snow angels and building improbable, lopsided snowmen. And with that many of us outdoors, shouting and laughing, we've declared the grounds safe from wolf attacks. Google assured us that lone wolves are most likely not going to approach a boisterous group of people and that they prefer to hunt at night, anyway.

I feel guilty at letting Mom do all the heavy lifting while we're outside playing. But she and Riven's dad have banned everyone from the kitchen and insisted on doing all the preparations by themselves. For someone who didn't want to get in the Christmas spirit, I haven't seen Mom so cheery since before we got the news Dad was sick.

"Do you think Mom has a crush on Riven's dad?" I ask Amy as we pull the twins around the yard in the saucer sleds we found in the tool shack. We've attached two ropes to them as not to break our backs bending forward, and the little ones are having a blast staring at the world from ground level. They're also too cute in their matching puffed-up snow suits.

"What makes you say that?" Amy asks.

I look through the house's wide French windows at Mom and Grant cooking together. "I don't know, she seems so brilliant around him, and was she wearing makeup this morning?"

"Yep, she asked for my lip gloss."

"And you didn't think it was odd?"

"No, I thought it was fantastic. If Mom's flirting with Mr.

Clark, I'm happy for her. She needs to have fun, and he seems like a perfect gentleman. Not to mention he's easy on the eyes for a silver fox." Amy throws me a mischievous side stare. "You know what they say?"

"No?"

"Like father…"

"What's that supposed to mean?"

"Only that his son is pretty handsome, too, in case you hadn't noticed. How's the room sharing going?"

I hope my cheeks are already red enough from the cold that she won't notice how hard I'm blushing. "Bunk beds are very uncomfortable."

"So, you don't like Riven Clark, the handsome writer genius, not even a bit?"

"I have a boyfriend."

Amy winces, a standard reaction.

"And anyway, we're staying only four more days. You know I don't have flings."

Amy scowls at me amiably. "If Mom can have a fling, then maybe you should, too."

"Mom is single, she can have all the flings she wants."

"Mom's having a fling?" Joshua repeats appearing out of nowhere.

Amy leans into him conspiratorially. "We suspect she has a crush on Mr. Clark, Senior."

"Oh, well." Joshua shrugs with the emotional depth typical of a twenty-something dude. "She sent me out to tell everyone we should get showered and changed, 'cause lunch is going to be ready in about an hour."

Amy and I dutifully follow the directive and drag the twins up to the porch steps, each picking one up once the saucer sleds hit the hard wood. The babies laugh happily all along.

"You need help to get them ready?"

"No, you go ahead," she says, taking her other son from me and stepping into the house. "And, Wendy?"

"Yes?"

"Wear some makeup, won't you?"

Amy winks at me and disappears up the stairs.

***

Half an hour later, I'm standing in front of the mirror with my makeup bag open on the sink, trying to decide what to put on. I don't want to be too obvious, but I also want to be pretty.

For Riven?

My heart kicks as I realize that, yes, I want to be pretty for him.

In the end, I opt for mild contouring, foundation, blusher, plain lip gloss, and a ton of mascara to make my eyes go POW! I blow-dry my hair and style it in soft waves that I let loose on my shoulders over the last cream-white wool sweater I found in my suitcase.

I wink at my reflection. Not bad!

Still, as I walk down the stairs, I feel ridiculously self-conscious for someone attending a Christmas family meal. Except my family won't be the only one at the table, so...

I keep my eyes low and make a beeline for my room to drop off the old clothes and makeup bag. No socks on the knob, I note, blushing.

Except Riven is in the room—fully dressed, unfortunately. I mean, luckily.

"Oh, hey," I say.

He turns to look at me and his eyes widen. He does his best to keep his features under wrap, but when he tries to talk a strangled noise comes out instead, and he has to cough and then try again. "Hey."

Definitely noticed the makeup, I note with satisfaction. I know it's silly, but knowing I have the power to destabilize a man like him—handsome, successful, genial—is exhilarating. Does he like me?

And then I can't help but wonder how this vacation would've gone if I were single. Which I'm not... therefore, I shouldn't indulge in wishful thinking. It's pointless.

When my gaze drops to his chest, I have to fight hard not to laugh. He's wearing a pale green ugly Christmas sweater with a stylized emerald fir tree taking up all his torso where the balls on the tree are real 3D puffs of faux fur.

"Cute sweater."

Riven looks down at his chest, then back up. "It's a longstanding Clark tradition to come to the Christmas meal in ugly-wear. This year I had a leg up; Park City is ten leagues ahead of LA in everything Christmas."

"Do you think it's because you Californians don't get the snow?"

He shrugs. "Could be? I mean, could you imagine a version of *Home Alone* set in LA instead of Chicago?"

I make an outraged face. "Nuuuuh, never."

"Exactly."

I awkwardly side-step him to drop my things in my case. As an afterthought, I fish my perfume out of the beauty case and covertly spray my neck while crouching down over the open suitcase.

"Well, then," I say, standing up. "I'll see you on the other side."

Nineteen

Riven

Enveloped in a cloud of Wendy's intoxicating perfume, I watch her exit the room, closing my hand in a tight fist and bringing it to my mouth to bite down on it.

She's wearing all white again. Either white is her favorite color, or she's doing it on purpose. And her face—today she looks even more gorgeous than usual. The woman is trying to kill me, slowly roasting me on a stick.

I should run outside and lie down in the snow for a couple of hours to cool down. Instead, I take a deep breath and exit the room. At least in the common areas, there'll be enough people to place a buffer between us. I study the open space, making a mental note of all the spots where they hung mistletoe to avoid them. If I have to kiss her again, it might be my tipping point. I'd go insane.

At lunchtime, I strategically sit on the opposite end of the table to Wendy, but on the same side, to dodge any risk of meeting her eyes. Maybe this way I'll be able to keep my wits about me.

The meal is huge. Dad and Emily prepared a feast, combining the best family recipes from our two clans. An assortment of crostini appetizers, the unmissable turkey with three different gravy sauces as the main dish, but also a turkey roulade for the kids, and a sort of round pie that Amy informs me is her mom's secret Choux crown recipe.

The number of sides is as impressive. From the classic mashed potatoes to a cranberry-apple relish, roasted beet-and-squash salad, and even mac and cheese, initially intended for the kids, but much appreciated by the adults as well. The desserts are no less majestic. Pumpkin pecan pie, caramelized apples, chocolate chip cake, and raspberry tarts.

We sit at the table for hours, eating, chatting, laughing. The two families intermingled. Clarks next to Nicholses. A far cry from that first lunch in town where we'd separated into two clear factions.

When the food runs out, at last, Wendy offers to help do the dishes. Instead of offering to help her, I station myself by the fireplace on fire duty. Once the kitchen is cleaned, we all reassemble in the living room to watch a movie—we opt for the new *Home Alone*. Most of us have to sit on the floor, leaning against various pieces of furniture for support, and again, I position myself on the opposite end of the living room from Wendy.

Home Sweet Home Alone isn't a long movie, but by the end, half the room is dozing off. I'm pretty drowsy myself. Both kids and adults opt to go to bed ridiculously early, which is actually a good thing since tomorrow we plan another day on the slopes.

I wait for my turn to use the upstairs bathroom, and when Tess comes out, I pull my sister into a bear hug.

"Oh my," she says as she hugs me in return. "What's this for?"

I lean back to look at her. "Thanks for forcing Christmas on me. You were right, the Clarks never skip. I would've been a miserable sod if I'd spent the day by myself."

"Ah, big brother." Tess gently taps me on the shoulders. "When will you learn that your sister is always right?"

"My sister who? The one with the really big head," I say, and before she can protest, I hug her again and add, "and an even bigger heart. Thank you."

"You're welcome." Tess gives me a kiss on the cheek and ruffles my hair. "Night."

"Night."

I take my time in the bathroom, but when I get downstairs to my shared bedroom, Wendy is still awake. She's in bed, checking her phone.

"Hey." She lifts her eyes as I enter the room. "I feel like I haven't seen you all day."

Oh, so she's noticed.

"I was the one at the end of the table busy stealing all the kids' food."

She laughs. "That's why the mac and cheese never reached my side."

I grin like an idiot. "Sorry, not sorry."

"Careful, Clark, you're tempting me to put salt in your coffee again."

"You promised you'd never ever do that again."

Wendy shrugs. "Then perhaps I'll use gravy."

I make a mock gag expression. "Please, no, the mere thought is disgusting enough." I mock gag again.

She raises an eyebrow. "So, you'll be a good boy?"

I have to. Especially since you've no idea how much of a bad boy I'd like to be now.

I nod at her and wish her goodnight, sinking into my bunk. Thankfully, I'm too stuffed to dwell. I just want to sleep and digest.

***

Come morning, I wake up well-rested and, surprisingly, with a good appetite.

Unfortunately, my attraction to Wendy is back with a vengeance, too. Especially when I see her geared up for the slopes. I'm pretty sure puffy ski suits aren't supposed to make women sexy, but with Wendy, I've given up and accepted that she could wear a potato sack and still take my breath away.

At least today I'll be able to channel my restlessness into physical exertion, flexing my muscles on the snow. Without meaning to, I end up coupling up with Wendy again. We race each other down the slopes all day with almost no interruptions. Since no one is that hungry after yesterday's huge meal, the group barely stops for lunch and we ski well into the afternoon.

At four, when the others all quit for the day, Wendy begs me to do one last run with her.

It's getting dark pretty fast, but I don't have it in me to say no to her. We catch literally the last chairlift up, but when we arrive on top an unwelcome surprise awaits us: a thick cloud has engulfed the mountain peak, making it impossible to see past our noses.

We get off the chair and Wendy turns left. I follow her, calling, "Wendy, wait. Stop!"

She halts at the edge of the slope. And I know she's looking at me questioningly, even if I can't exactly see her eyes underneath her mirrored goggles.

"We should go the other way," I say, catching up with her.

"What? The beginner run? No."

I lift my sunglasses and she does the same. "Come on, Wendy. The visibility is awful."

"It's not that bad, and I'm sure it's just a cloud at the top. It's going to clear out soon."

"You can't be sure." I shake my head. "It isn't safe."

"This could be my last run of the season," Wendy pouts. "The weather forecast for the next two days is horrible and we're leaving the day after."

My heart twists at the casualty with which she talks about leaving. But I ignore the metaphysical matter of her imminent departure to concentrate on the practical aspects of getting down this mountain.

"Wendy—"

"Don't Wendy me."

"I'm not Wendying you, I'm just saying that it's the end of the day, the visibility is crap, and the terrain uneven. We should go the other way."

Wendy pulls her goggles back on and smirks at me. "Suit yourself, but the last one at the bottom is a looooooser."

She launches down the slope.

That damn woman will be the death of me. I pull my sunglasses back on and follow her downhill.

Follow is not the right word because I can't see her in all this fog. I have to proceed cautiously, mostly blindly down one of the hardest runs of the resort. As expected, the terrain is a nasty mix of moguls, sections with wet, heavy snow, as well as icy and slippery patches.

A total nightmare.

At least with the snowboard, I don't risk having one ski sinking in mushy snow while the other slips on a slate of ice. The thought has barely crossed my mind when the fog finally clears and I spot Wendy ending up exactly in that situation.

One of her skis gets stuck in a mound of fresh powder while the other slides forward on a slab of ice and hardened snow.

She tumbles down, hitting the ground face first, and then does a couple of somersaults downhill while her skis and poles fly in opposite directions to the four cardinal points.

My heart stops in my chest as Wendy's fall comes to an abrupt end onto another mogul of soft snow and she doesn't get up.

I rush to her side, screeching to a stop beside her unmoving body. I can't unfasten my boots fast enough and I don't even care that, once I'm free, the snowboard slides downhill out of my reach, probably lost forever.

I drop to my knees next to Wendy's limp form and recoil at the amount of blood marring her face—too much blood. The warm liquid is soaking into the snow around her, forming a ruby-red pool.

I don't dare to touch her or move her. I dart a glance up the hill, but the view is still blocked by the cloud. No one will come down this way. No sane person would be that foolish.

"Damn you, Wendy."

I throw off my gloves and call 911.

Two mountain rescue snowmobiles reach us after the longest, most strenuous five minutes of my life. A paramedic gets off and kneels on Wendy's other side while the other picks up a walkie-talkie.

"Subject unconscious, we request immediate aerial support."

"We'll radio in for the helicopter," a metallic response comes through the walkie-talkie, disturbed by static.

"How is she?" I ask the man in front of me.

The paramedic has two fingers under Wendy's neck. "Pulse is good and strong, and I can't spot any clear injury."

"But where is all the blood coming from?"

"It could be just a nose bleed, sir, they look worse than they really are. But I can't be sure."

For the first time since I saw Wendy fall, I catch a breath and my pulse slows to only a thousand beats per minute instead of a million.

Soon a helicopter arrives. The paramedics carry Wendy aboard on a stretcher and the machine takes off again within minutes of landing. I shield my face from the storm of snow the helicopter blades kick up and, with my heart in my mouth, watch the red vehicle disappear among the darkening clouds.

"You need a ride downhill, sir?" the same paramedic who assisted Wendy asks me. He's already collected Wendy's skis and loaded them on the snowmobile.

"Yes, please," I reply. "I lost my board."

I mount on the snowmobile behind him and in no time, we reach the bottom of the slope.

Wendy's family is waiting for us next to mine, and when they see me dismount a rescue vehicle alone, the smiles are wiped from their faces. I wished nothing more than to tell them that everything is going to be all right, but the truth is, I don't know.

I give them the hard facts as I witnessed them. To their credit, no one panics. Wendy's mom asks the paramedic a few questions, but he can't provide any more answers than I could besides the hospital she's being flown to.

Once that information is received, the Nicholses get organized for the drive to Salt Lake City.

Amy is heartbroken she has to go home to take care of the twins and can't follow her sister to the hospital. But Wendy's mom and Joshua reassure her they'll give her constant updates.

Dad offers to accompany Emily. And I, too, join them.

The ride to Salt Lake Regional Medical Center is grim, and the wait at the hospital is even bleaker. The minutes trickle by unbearably slow, leaving me plenty of time to mentally berate myself. I should've insisted more. I should've put my foot down and said we were going down the beginner slope, full stop. Or even better, I shouldn't have agreed to the last run.

After what seems like ages, a doctor finally comes to the waiting room to give us an update on Wendy's condition.

Twenty

Wendy

In a stunned haze, I open my eyes, trying to understand where I am or why my head is hurting so much.

Correction, I open only one eye because the other seems to be stuck under some sort of bandage. I touch my hand to it. An eye patch?

To my right, a monitor is beeping regularly and, on my left, Riven is slouched in an armchair, asleep.

I'm at the hospital.

Why? What happened? And why is Riven in the room with me? Where's my family?

Some sort of sixth sense must signal to him that I'm awake because he jolts upright and blinks at me.

Then he smiles—a full, ten-million-megawatt smile.

"Hey," he says, his voice still low and groggy with sleep. "You're up."

I repeat aloud all the questions I just asked myself. "Why am I in the hospital? What happened? Why are you in my room? Where's my family?"

Riven's smile lightens up still. "Woah, Nichols, you go from zero to 100. Glad to have you back."

"What am I doing in the hospital?" I repeat.

"Well, you had a pretty spectacular fall on the last run. They had to call a helicopter just for you." He shrugs. "Not a surprise considering how high maintenance you are." His lips twitch.

"I fell?"

"Right on a slab of ice, face first."

My hand goes back to my bandaged eye. "And my eye?"

"The short answer is that it's going to be okay, but I'm not a doctor and I can't remember any of the fancy words they used to say that. Also, I kind of spaced out after they said you'd be all right."

I bite on a fingernail. "That bad, uh?"

"You gave us a horrible scare, Captain Hook."

I raise my one free eyebrow. "Hook?"

"Yeah, from Peter Pan, Wendy Darling, the eye patch suits you."

I narrow one eye at him. "Why are *you* in my room? Where's my family?"

"Well, Amy had to take care of the twins and couldn't come. Your mom wanted to spend the night, but this chair would've probably destroyed her back." He stretches like a cat. "It sure killed mine. And once it became clear you weren't in any mortal danger, Joshua didn't offer to stay, so I did. Roommate pact, I guess."

He says it casually, but my lower lip starts to quiver dangerously. I take one deep breath and study him. "That's it?"

"Did I forget any of your questions?"

"No, I'm waiting for the huge 'I told you so' and the following when-I-say-the-expert-run-is-too-dangerous-you-should-listen-to-me pep talk."

"Ah, no memory loss, that's a good sign." Riven leans forward, elbows on his knees. "Don't worry, Hook, you get a pass this time."

I nod. "Sorry," I say. "And thank you for spending the night with me. You can go rest now."

"Your mom said she'd come back as soon as she could. I'll wait." Riven checks his watch. "They should bring you breakfast shortly, but do you want me to get you anything from the vending machines? Coffee—with how much salt, again?"

I suppress a smile. "Actually, just water, I'm parched."

"Yeah, the doctors said you might be. A side effect of the anesthesia."

I goggle my one good eye. "Anesthesia?"

"Yeah, your retina. The eye surgeon had to do a procedure."

I'm about to ask for details when a nurse walks in with a tray of food. "You're awake, wonderful. And just in time for breakfast."

As soon as the nurse drops the tray in front of me, I open the water bottle and drain it in a few long gulps.

Riven smiles. "Should I go get another one?"

"Yes, please." He leaves the room, and I turn to the nurse, who's reading data from the monitors on my right and copying the numbers in my medical file. "Nurse, do you know what happened to my eye?"

She reads the top of the charts. "You had a retinal detachment, dear. The doctor will come to see you in a minute to explain everything. In the meantime, try not to worry. Dr. Curt is the best eye surgeon in the state."

"Thank you," I say.

The nurse nods and leaves the room just as Riven comes back with two bottles of water in his hands. "I know you prefer sparkling, but I wasn't sure if that counts also for post-op thirst."

My heart tugs. Two years after dating Brandon, I still have to correct him at restaurants when he tries to order regular water for both of us.

"Sparkling is great, thank you."

"Morning," a doctor in his mid-fifties says in a booming voice. He has a white mustache and a reassuring face. "How are we feeling this morning?"

"Thirsty," I reply, taking another long sip of water.

"Perfectly normal," he replies. "We usually carry out these procedures with local anesthesia, but given the—ah—traumatic nature of your injury, we preferred to put you out. Plus, you were half gone, anyway. Does your head hurt?"

"Yep."

"And your eye?"

I nod.

"Well, young lady, paracetamol is going to become your best friend for the next six to eight weeks. Other than that, I'm happy to report your surgery went by the manual, and you should suffer no long-term consequences. Perhaps a black eye for the next week or so."

"Can you explain exactly what the procedure was?"

"Sure. We had to perform a retinal reattachment surgery." Dr. Curt winks at me. "Not as scary as it sounds. The gist of it is that, because of your fall, a thin layer of tissue at the back of your eye, the retina, became loose. We had to get in there and repair the damage."

Not sure the answer will make me feel any better, I ask, "How?"

"We injected your eye with a gas bubble to push the detached retina back into place and then we reattached it with cryotherapy. No visible scars for you."

They usually do that with people *awake?* Now I'm glad I was passed out. I would've died of fear.

"Okay. When can I go home?"

The doctor smiles benevolently at me. "Ah, all patients' favorite question. We send retinal detachments home right away, but your scans also showed a slight concussion, so we'd rather enjoy your company for another night."

My shoulders relax with relief. "But I'll still be able to catch my flight home the day after tomorrow, right?"

For the first time, the doctor's brow furrows. "Afraid not, Miss Nichols. A pesky side effect of the surgery is a total embargo on flying for the entire recovery time."

I swallow. "But—but you said it'll take six to—"

"Six to eight weeks, correct."

"You mean, I'll have to *drive* home?"

"Where's home, miss?"

"New York."

"Ah."

I don't like the way he said *ah.*

The doctor takes a deep breath and I steady myself for the worst news, which he promptly delivers, "Miss Nichols, you're also forbidden to drive. Your sight won't be up to par for a while, sorry. And even if you found a kind soul who'd drive you the thirty-plus hours across the country, I'm afraid the car vibrations and constant stress to the retina would be detrimental to your eye recovery." He sighs. "If I were you, I'd concentrate on how to get comfortable in Salt Lake City for the next two months."

Twenty-one

Riven

Wendy is grounded. She's staying in Utah for another six to eight weeks. I take in the doctor's words with a mix of dread and elation. Next, I feel like a jerk for being even the slightest happy about Wendy smashing her face in the snow, having to undergo eye surgery, and then getting stuck away from home for two months. Away from her friends, from her work, from her lousy *boyfriend*...

Oh my gosh, I'm the worst.

The doctor leaves, and Wendy stares around the hospital chamber, utterly lost. When her free eye meets mine, she looks even more adrift.

I don't have time to offer any comforting words as her family arrives. Emily, Amy, Joshua, all enter the room alongside my dad. Dad and I leave the Nicholses alone to give them some privacy as they discuss Wendy's recovery and head to the hospital cafeteria. Me, to have breakfast, and Dad, for a coffee reinforcement.

I tell Dad the news Wendy will have to stay in Utah for the foreseeable future, and his lips twitch. But he's quick to hide the reaction and school his features in a stern, concerned line.

"Such a misfortune," he comments, shaking his head.

"Yep," I say, staring at my black coffee and thinking I need to ask Wendy what she puts in hers because, after tasting her vanilla version, black coffee simply doesn't do it for me anymore.

"You think they had enough time by themselves?" Dad asks after a while. "Should we go back?"

I nod. We collect our used plates and cups, sort them in the various recycling bins, and head upstairs.

In the room, the vibe isn't great. Wendy's cheeks are red and she looks like she's been crying. Emily has a concerned look on her face, and so does Amy. The only cool one seems to be Joshua.

"What's going on?" I ask him.

Wendy's brother shrugs. "We phoned the real estate agency, and Kelly Anne told us it's going to be tricky to find a decent place for Wendy, considering it's still tourist season and she needs to be within walking distance to pretty much everything since she can't drive."

"Nonsense," I say, looking directly at Wendy. "Of course, you can stay at the cabin with me."

"But—but wouldn't I crowd your space?"

"Wendy, there are currently sixteen people living in that house. It's going to feel like a palace with only the two of us." As I say the words, the magnitude of what I'm proposing strikes me. Two months in the same house with Wendy—with no buffers!

Well, at least there'll be separate rooms this time.

Emily comes to me with a look of sheer gratitude in her eyes. "Oh, Riven, would you really let our Wendy stay with you? I'd feel so much better if she had someone who could help her. She won't let me stay."

"Mom," Wendy shouts, embarrassed. "Riven doesn't need a half invalid in his way. He came to Park City to concentrate on his book. The last thing he needs is to drive me around whenever I have to go grocery shopping."

"Well," I say. "Believe it or not, novelists eat, too. We don't survive on our art exclusively. You can carpool with me when I go into town."

Wendy stares at me, her gaze simultaneously hopeful and worried—because of what living together for two months could do to us?

Stop building castles in the air, man, it wouldn't mean anything. She still has a boyfriend back home. Heck, he's probably flying down to visit her as soon as he learns about the accident. Oh gosh, and he'll expect to stay at the house with us. Does that mean I'll have to listen to them have actual sex now? Failed phone sex has been hard enough to stomach. I'm not sure I can cope with the real thing.

I involuntarily wince. Wendy must notice my grimace and interpret it the wrong way, because her lips take a stubborn curve and she says, "Don't worry, I don't need to be your charity case."

What a pig-headed, mulish thing to say. "Wendy, I'd be happy to do it." *Too* happy, perhaps, I comment in my head. "We've become friends, right? This is what friends do."

She opens her mouth to say something, but her mom steps in. "Either you stay with Riven or I'm staying in Utah with you for the next two months, and you know your sister relies on me a lot to help with the kids."

Amy nods in the background.

Wendy closes her mouth and stares at us until finally, she gives a small, almost imperceptible nod, adding, "But I'm paying half the rent and that's nonnegotiable."

I smile. "I can live with that."

It's the rest I'm not sure about.

Twenty-two

Wendy

I'm ashamed at how relieved I am when Riven offers to let me stay with him. The thought of having to go house hunting during peak season was daunting. And the prospect of spending the next two months living with my mom was something I couldn't cope with. I love Mom, but I'm not a teenager anymore and one thing she's never been able to stop doing is *mothering*.

I hope Riven really meant it when he said he wants me to stay at the cabin. That he's not just doing it out of pity... But he insisted so much. And he said we're friends.

Friends... I mull over the word. Somehow, the term doesn't satisfy me. Why? Do I want us to be *more* than friends?

Don't go there, Wendy. The fact that you're staying for two months changes nothing, it only shifted the duration of your acquaintance with Riven. But once your eye recovers, you'll still be living in New York, and he'll still be in LA. Plus, you already have a boyfriend.

Right, Brandon!

Has anyone told him about the accident?

After I manage to send my family home with the request that they please enjoy their last day of vacation with multiple reassurances that, yes, I can take care of myself for a day in a hospital full of nurses ready to assist me, I recover my phone and dial Brandon's number.

"Hello..."

"Hey Bra—"

"Hello? ... hello? ... Just Kidding, leave me a message."

"Aaargh," I scream, having to do my best not to haul the phone at the wall.

I hang up without leaving a message and text him instead.

> I had an accident, I'm at the hospital

> Please call me back as soon as you read this

For once, he doesn't make me wait and calls right away.

"Babe," he says. "What happened? Are you okay?"

I tell him about the fall and the retina reattachment, and then I add, "The thing is, I can't fly back home so soon after the surgery. I'll have to stay in Utah for a while."

"For how long exactly?" Brandon asks, his tone wary.

"Six to eight weeks the doctor said."

"Uh, yeah, uh, I'm sorry, babe, thing is—"

"No, don't worry, a friend has offered to host me and maybe you could come visit one weekend—"

"I don't think so," Brandon cuts me off. "When I said I was sorry, I meant about us..."

"Us? What do you mean?"

"Yeah, I don't do long distance."

What is he talking about? "Brandon, this is only temporary. I'll be gone two months, tops."

"No, I get it, but my job is too stressful to go without sex for two months. A week was already a stretch."

Oh my gosh, the meaning of his words sinks in. "Are you breaking up with me?"

The line stays silent for a moment. "Unless you want to try an open relationship while you're over there…"

"Like you want to have sex with other women while I'm gone and I should be okay with that?"

"Hey, I'm trying to be as honest as I can, babe. Lots of dudes would've just cheated on you without saying a word."

Oh, lucky me, what a true gentleman you are, Brandon, I mentally scoff, while my mouth gapes open and I blink, unable to reply.

"I guess that's a no, then," he says. "Well, sorry about your fall. Call me when you get back to the city. Gotta get back to work now. Take care."

Brandon hangs up, and I sink on the pillows of my hospital bed, clasping my phone in my hands while something inside of me breaks. No, not my heart. But perhaps my self-esteem, my sense of self-worth.

Why did I waste two years of my life on this guy? Why does no man ever care about me? Why has no one ever fallen head over heels in love with me? All men ever wanted from me was to have fun in bed for a while, and when they get tired, they move on as if I never existed.

What is wrong with me?

Feeling numb, I close my eyes. I'm too tired to consider any of those questions. That's it, I'm done fighting or searching for love. I don't care anymore.

I don't care about anything.

Twenty-three
Riven

Five days later

I circle the couch, taking in Wendy's half-reclined form and wondering what my next move should be. Our families have left three days ago, and ever since, she hasn't moved from that couch except for the occasional bathroom break or to go to sleep in the attic bedroom.

Every day, she follows the same routine. She sleeps until noon or later. When she comes downstairs, she flops on the couch and turns on the TV. She's cycling through all ten seasons of *Friends* on demand.

Food doesn't seem to interest her. She nibbles on whatever I bring her, leaving most behind.

She refused to celebrate the New Year. Not that I had this grand feast in mind, but a simple toast at midnight would've been nice. We could've watched the city's fireworks from the upstairs balcony together. Instead, at nine, she was already in bed.

She has been subdued ever since coming back from the hospital, but things have deteriorated since her family left. As long as they were here, she made an effort to act normal around them. But now that they've gone, she's blanked out.

Amy told me Wendy's boyfriend broke up with her over the phone, but I don't know the details. No one has been able to get Wendy to talk about it. Gosh, she must've really been into the guy if this is her reaction.

That dude, how?

I would've thought she'd be more relieved than sad to be rid of him. But for the breakup to cause such a backlash...

I have some experience with how women react to heartbreak. Like that time in high school when Tess was dating Johnny Clever, the football team quarterback and most popular guy in school, and then found out he had two more girlfriends in two other schools. She spent an entire week crying and eating ice cream out of the carton with her girlfriends. But at least my sister was *reacting* in some way. Wendy has just gone totally passive.

Her phone pings. Wendy glances fleetingly at the screen but doesn't reach for it to read or answer the text.

Not being able to communicate with her, her family has been asking me for updates on her well-being. So far, I've covered for her, making up excuses—she sleeps a lot, the phone screen is too bright, she can't read very well yet—pretending she's given me messages to pass on. But I don't know how much longer I can keep up the pretense, or how long I should.

"Wendy," I call out now. "I'm making lunch. Anything you're in the mood for?"

Without detaching her gaze from the TV screen, she replies, "Whatever you're having is fine."

Of course, she'd say that. I've already tried leaving her without food, but she just got up from the couch to grab a banana from the fruit basket and that was her dinner. She can't survive on fruit. I've also considered emptying the cupboards and fridge of all food to see what her reaction would be, but I'm honestly scared she'd simply not eat. And so far, keeping her on a healthy, albeit scant, diet is the only thing I've succeeded at, so I won't stop now.

What can I cook? What did we have yesterday? Pasta for lunch and tacos for dinner. I open the fridge, searching for inspiration. Burgers? Nah. I have tomatoes, mozzarella cheese… A Caprese salad? Uhm, tasty, healthy, but I'm in the mood for something warm. Almond chicken? No, I made it the other day. A two-pack of salmon filets catches my eyes.

Bingo.

If my honey-glazed grilled salmon doesn't resuscitate her from the dead, nothing will.

Thirty minutes later, I present Wendy with the most inviting, crisped to culinary perfection dish. Only I make the mistake of lingering too long in front of the TV screen as I serve it to her. She takes the plate from me and cranes her neck to stare at the TV past me.

"Why don't you join me at the table?"

"No, thanks, I'm good on the couch. Would you mind?" She makes a move-aside gesture.

I leave her to her stupid TV show and go eat my lunch alone at the kitchen bar.

Mmm… delicious.

Wendy must not agree because when I go to collect her plate from the coffee table in front of the couch, she's barely grazed a third of the salmon and the side vegetables look untouched.

"You didn't like it?" I ask. "I can make you something else."

"No, it was great. I'm just not hungry, thank you."

I take the plate and drop it in the sink.

Okay, the carrot clearly isn't working—time to bring out the stick.

Twenty-four

Wendy

"I'm going into town," Riven says, grabbing his car keys and putting on his parka. "You want to come?"

"No," I say, thinking I want to finish my days on this couch, talking to as few people as I can manage.

"You need me to bring you anything?"

"No, thanks, I'm good."

"See you later," Riven opens the front door, letting in a draft of chilly air, and then bangs the door shut as he goes out.

I snuggle further under my plaid blanket and concentrate on the *Friends* episode, *The One Where Everybody Finds Out*.

Riven comes back five episodes later. That's how I'm marking the passing of time now, in *Friends* episodes.

He drops a bag of groceries on the kitchen counter and stores the fresh produce in the fridge while I brace myself for the next attempt he'll make at making conversation or trying to have me move from the couch.

I don't understand why he won't just let me be. The doctor prescribed plenty of rest; I'm just following instructions.

Thankfully, Riven doesn't say a word as he puts away the groceries and then disappears upstairs. After a few minutes, I hear the water running. He must be taking a shower.

But too soon afterward for him to have showered, he comes back down the stairs. Riven crosses the living room and plants himself squarely in front of the TV, blocking my view.

I shift sides on the couch to keep watching, but Riven grabs the remote control and turns the TV off.

"Hey," I protest. "I was watching that."

"Sorry, Wendy, but this is an intervention."

"An intervention, why? I'm perfectly fine."

"Because, trust me, you don't want to make that saying about houseguests and fish true."

I frown. Fish, houseguests, what is he talking about? Then the Benjamin Franklin quote comes to mind: *houseguests, like fish, begin to smell after three days.*

Is he saying I smell? I take a covert sniff under my armpit and, okay, it isn't exactly fresh, but it doesn't *smell* either.

I look up at him, outraged. "I don't smell and I'm not a houseguest, I'm paying half the rent."

"Still, you haven't showered in three days."

"The doctor said I can't shower until he removes the bandage."

"But he said nothing about you not taking a bath. I ran one for you in the master suite." Riven eyes my head dubiously. "I bet if you're careful you can even wash your hair."

When I refuse to engage further or stand up, Riven points his thumb at the stairs. "The bath isn't optional, Wendy. Go before the water gets cold and then, if you want, you can spend the rest of your life on this couch."

I throw the blanket away from my body and stand up. "Yes, *Mom.* Gosh, I should've asked my real mother to stay, she would've been less annoying than you."

Unmoved, Riven points at the stairs again, so I have no other choice than to stomp upstairs, sulking.

In the bathroom, I consider locking myself in for twenty minutes to pretend I've bathed, but the tub looks really inviting, all steamy and bubbly. Did he even put salts in the water? It's too blue to be natural. I check the temperature with a finger, still hot. Okay, Mr. Nosy, you win.

I take my sweats off and sink in. The warmth immediately wraps around my every limb, massaging my atrophied muscles after three days of couch living. I enjoy the sensation for a few minutes and then, careful not to get my eye or the bandage wet, I lean my head backward until my hair is completely submerged. When I reemerge, I search for shampoo. On the corner of the tub, there are only a purple bottle, a pink jar of the same brand, and a white comb. I grab the bottle and read the label:

Violet Crush for Blondes, Purple shampoo. Neutralizes stubborn brassy tones in one use for cooler, brighter blonde.

This must be a leftover from Amy's stay in the master suite. My sister is notorious for being a beauty products junkie. She always uses the best brands.

I grab the shampoo and massage it on my scalp. Mmm… it smells heavenly, I can already feel my hair getting softer. Once again careful not to let a drop of water hit my face, I rinse the shampoo away. And I should be done, I should get out… but that pink jar is calling to me. It must be a hair mask. I grab it to make sure.

"Restore repair mask," I read aloud. "Deeply nourishes and reverses damage."

Well, of course it'd say something like that. I'm about to put it back, not sure I want to even bother when my eye falls on the white price tag still attached to the lid.

"Forty bucks," I exclaim out loud. "For a hair mask?"

Amy sure doesn't pinch any pennies when it comes to hair care.

Well, now I *have* to try it. I can't let a forty-buck hair mask go to waste.

I read the instructions:

After shampooing, apply generously from roots to ends.
Leave in place for twenty minutes. Rinse thoroughly.

Twenty minutes? How does Amy even find the time to take twenty-minute showers with four kids?

On the contrary, I'm childless and will die a spinster… so I have all the time in the world.

I shrug and open the jar. The inside is a pearlescent pink color and smells of coconut and shea butter. I pick up a generous dollop and use the comb to comb it through my hair. I repeat the process until all my hair is covered and gently massage the mask into the ends to let it sink in better. That's where the worst damage is, anyway. Once I'm satisfied, I twist my hair in a high bun over my head and set a timer on my phone.

I add more hot water to the bath and lay my head backward, ready for a twenty-minute nap.

When the timer goes off, it feels like I've barely closed my eyes. But the water has gone lukewarm, so it must've really been twenty minutes—a whole *Friends* episode.

I use the tub spray to rinse the mask away. The water comes out a pretty pink color, and soon the entire tub is pink. Using my toes, I lift the plug and let all the pink water wash away. I keep rinsing, contorting in various positions as not to wet my eye until the water returns transparent, and, combing a hand through my hair, I don't sense any residual product.

To avoid any wayward droplets sneaking down my forehead while I finish showering, I grab a white towel from the stool next to the tub and collect my wet hair in a turban.

There's no shower gel. Ah. Mr. Perfect downstairs forgot something. I shrug and grab the purple shampoo—it's still soap. Once I'm properly showered, I step out of the tub and wrap myself in the clean, folded bathrobe Riven has prepared for me.

The bathroom looks like a Turkish bath by now, all foggy with vapor. The windows and mirror are completely opaque with condensation. I search the cabinets for a blow dryer and after giving my hair one last rub with the towel, I dry it, blowing it backward, away from my face to avoid getting hot air in my eye. I usually prefer to do this with my head upside down, but the doctor forbade it.

With the first layer of dampness gone, I point the blow dryer at the mirror to have a better view of what I'm doing. But once my reflection appears, I stare back at it dumbfounded for a second, until an inhuman scream rips from my throat.

Twenty-five

Riven

The scream that ripples through the house from the upstairs bathroom would be worthy of any respectable horror movie.

"Here we go," I mutter, folding the newspaper I've been reading.

I stand up from the couch and brace myself for the incoming storm. Promptly, the bathroom door bangs open, and angry steps stomp down the stairs.

I move behind the couch to put a barrier of sorts between me and the approaching fury.

Wendy storms into the living room, still wearing only a bathrobe and pointing a finger at me.

Don't be distracted, Riven, not even by the tantalizing amount of legs-skin exposed.

"You did this!" she yells. "The nice bath, the speech, it was all a ploy."

No point in denying it, summoning my most smartass expression I shrug. "It worked."

"What do you mean *it worked?*"

"You're off the couch and showing signs of a personality."

"My hair is pink!" Wendy screams. "My perfect, natural, never-dyed hair is freaking *pink!*"

Wendy starts to reach for me, but I circle the couch keeping it firmly between us. "Technically, the shade is pearl blush—"

"Tell me it's washable or I swear I'll strangle you with my bare hands."

"It's washable."

Wendy stops circling around the couch trying to catch me and narrows her one free eye at me. "Is it really?"

"No, sorry, the hair salon only had permanent dye. But they assured me this color is really hip."

"The hair salon? You went to a hair salon specifically to substitute Amy's hair mask with pink dye, why?"

"Actually, both the shampoo and the fake hair mask come from the hair salon, but yes, I asked them to put the pink dye in the mask container, and I correctly anticipated you'd assume those were Amy's leftovers and help yourself."

"But why? Why did you do this to me?"

"I couldn't get you to react in any other way, so making you mad seemed like my best last option." I smirk, crossing my arms over my chest. "You're welcome."

"Oh, so I should thank you now? You're completely deranged. And react to what, anyway? I was absolutely fine!"

"Wendy, you've been catatonic for days. You weren't answering your family or your friends, you've barely been talking to me—"

"That's because you're clearly a sociopath." She pulls on a string of hair as if demonstrating her theory.

"And you weren't eating or showering, what was I supposed to do?"

Wendy grips the couch cushions. "*Not* dye my hair pink. My hair is freaking pink."

"Yeah, I think we've established that. But you looked like you were sinking into depression, and I was worried."

"My whole life has fallen apart," she hisses. "I've nearly lost an eye, I'm stuck in the middle of nowhere for two months, and my boyfriend of two years broke up with me over the phone because his job is too stressful to go six weeks without sex." *Ah, so these are the sordid breakup details.* I only have a moment to take them in before Wendy keeps yelling at me, "I was doing what every normal person would do—taking a few days to lick my wounds in peace."

"Bullshit. You looked like you'd lost all will to live. Heck, my wife of seven years dumped me for a soap opera buff and I wasn't *that* down."

Wendy's face doesn't register any surprise at my revelation. Did she know already I'm going through a divorce? Has she looked into me? I don't have time to reflect on these questions as her reaction to my confession leaves me perplexed.

"Ha... ha, ha, ha..." Wendy lets out a hysterical laugh. "You're priceless."

"What's so funny about my divorce?"

"That you call bullshit on me when you're the one full of shit!" Her voice rises a few octaves.

"Meaning?"

"I was having a three-day mini-breakdown, yes, okay. It would've lasted a week, tops, while you've been hiding in this cabin in the middle of nowhere for how many months now?"

"I'm not hiding, I'm trying to finish a book while my house is undergoing renovations."

"BULLSHIT," Wendy screams. "If my hair is pink yours should be electric blue."

"Let's go down to the salon and have them dye it then. If it'll get you out of the house."

She throws her arms up in the air. "You're impossible, and my hair is pink..." the last word comes out as half a sob, then her shoulders begin to shake and she starts crying, only it soon turns into laughing until I can't tell which one it is anymore.

"If it's any consolation, the pink looks really great on you."

The cry-laughing increases in intensity.

"Hey, I got you something." I throw the small package at her from across the couch as I still don't feel safe getting any closer to her. "Catch."

Wendy catches it, and I'm impressed. I mean she can only use one eye and even that one must have blurred vision with all those tears.

She looks up at me, chest still heaving. "W-What is it?"

"Open it."

She pulls the strings of the green velvet drawstring purse and takes out the cute pink eye patch I bought her to match the hair.

The cry-laughing turns into solid laughing as Wendy shakes her head. "You're really impossible."

"You should go get dressed before you catch a cold."

And before I lose my sanity, I add in my head.

All that chasing around the living room has made the bathrobe neckline perilously low and the slit has risen almost to the juncture in her thighs.

Wendy stares down at herself and immediately closes up the gaps, pulling the bathrobe so tightly around her body it covers her, neck to calves.

She comes over to my side of the couch and for once I don't flee, only take a precautionary step back. "You're not forgiven." Wendy rises that adorable accusatory finger at me. "You owe me, big time."

"Big time," I agree. "Anything I can do for you right away?"

Wendy sighs. "Please make pancakes, I'm starving."

"It's three in the afternoon."

"So?" she asks challengingly.

"Pancakes it is, ma'am."

Wendy nods and tromps up the stairs, making a point of keeping her chin held high.

I shake my head, smiling. I head to the fridge to take out the eggs and milk.

Before closing the door, my eyes land on the half beetroot left over from the beetroot risotto I made the other day.

I grab it just because I'm a jerk, and because I think Captain Hook really deserves pink pancakes to go with her new hairstyle.

Twenty-six

Wendy

Upstairs, I stare in the mirror, trying to make an objective appraisal of the hair situation. The color isn't bad per se, it's just so not me. I've always been a blonde. And pink is such a bold color.

Well, I'd better get used to it. I don't want to bleach my hair back to blonde and fry it. Thank goodness I have two entire months to adjust to the new style before I have to face anyone I know.

I finish styling the soft curls and comb through them. For hair that has just been dyed it feels incredibly soft. At least Riven went to a proper hair salon to get the dye and not to the dollar store. That he'd dare do such a thing still makes me pretty incensed, but a tiny part of me can also see his point. For the past few days, I've been out of it. Still, I wouldn't go as far as calling it depression.

As I let my hair fall down below my shoulders, I can't stop staring. Not bad, except maybe for the white gauze eye patch, which is a bit of an eyesore—pun intended. I grab Riven's pink patch and put it on.

Great, I'm a very cool pirate. Pity Halloween was two months ago.

I pick up my phone to take a selfie and I'm surprised at the 247 unanswered notifications awaiting an answer in the messaging app next to the camera. Basically, everyone I know has been writing to me, and I've ignored them all for three days straight.

I'll have to check and reply to all messages, but for now, I only pick up the chat with Mindy, scroll past her millions of *'are you okay, where are you, what's happening, why aren't you picking up your phone'* texts, and I snap a selfie and send it to her.

Her reply comes in immediately.

> Oh, thank goodness you're alive!

> And your hair is pink!

> Explain yourself

>> Riven thought I was getting depressed over the breakup with Brandon and the accident and since he couldn't get at me in any other way, he decided to make me mad

>> He tricked me into dyeing my hair pink and bought me a matching eye patch

>> FYI, the dye is non-washable

Please marry the guy

He's my personal hero

Be serious

I am being serious

Drop your phone and go propose to that man

A) I'm not even sure if his divorce is final. And B) we never even properly kissed, what if there's no chemistry?

A) there are ways to find out. And B) there are even better ways to find out

I ignore her innuendo and bring the subject back to my hair.

No, seriously, what do you think of the hair? Is it hideous?

It's the coolest thing I've ever seen

The screen lights up with an incoming call from my mom. I can't keep ignoring her, so I text Mindy a quick apology:

Sorry, I have to go

My mom is calling and I haven't picked up in three days

She's probably going crazy

Talk soon

You'd better

Disappear on me again and I'll shave your head

I won't, pinky promise

And Wendy? You're single now, time to have fun

I don't reply and pick up instead. "Hi, Mom."

"Wendy! You picked up. I'd lost hope. I was about to book a flight to come check on you. I mean, Riven said you were doing okay, but no one had heard from you in days."

"You've talked to Riven?"

"Yes, when you weren't picking up, we called him."

"And he said I was okay?"

"Yes, why? Are you *not* okay?" she sounds alarmed again.

So, not only he fed me for three days while stoically putting up with my horrible attitude, but he also covered for me with my family.

"Sure, I'm okay. I was just exhausted," I lie. "Must've been the anesthesia. I slept almost the entire time."

"And is Riven taking good care of you?"

I glance at the pink hair in the mirror. Admit it or not, I sort of needed a jolt. "The best care. He's been a fantastic friend."

"Of course, of course, it's just we didn't hear from you, and we didn't know what to think—"

"I'm fine, Mom, I promise. You don't need to worry, okay?"

"Okay. But please reply also to your brother and sister. They've been worried sick as well."

I doubt a text from Joshua is even in the 247 unread ones I got, but I reassure Mom I'll notify every last relative of my well-being.

I delete all the useless messages on my phone since I don't need to read 247 variations of *how are you* and simply shoot the whole family a message in our group chat reassuring all my contacts that I'm alive and well.

In my room, I change into something more sophisticated than sweats. Even if I don't plan on leaving the house today, I still want to give myself a better look. Then I collect all the dirty clothes I've scattered around the floor in a huge tote bag and head downstairs.

After I gorge on Riven's sure-to-be-delicious pancakes, laundry will be my top priority. I brought enough changes for a week, and I'm running out fast, even if my mom preemptively washed everything for me before leaving. Tomorrow, I'll need to head into town to shop for new clothes. And I also need to plan my revenge. Riven might think he had a point tricking me into dyeing my hair pink, but the prank won't go unanswered.

Twenty-seven

Riven

When I come down the stairs the next morning, Wendy is already in the kitchen making coffee. She's wearing jeans and a wool knit sweater, gray with a red-and-white pattern across her collarbone.

"Early rise?" I ask, surprised but pleased.

"We have a busy day," she replies cryptically.

"We?"

Wendy hands me a cup of coffee with a smile as sweet as arsenic. "Coffee?"

I take the mug and smell it suspiciously. I can't detect any salt, but then again, I couldn't the last time, either.

Wendy stares at me expectantly. "Something the matter?"

"No," I say. If drinking salted coffee is the price I have to pay to see her smile again, I'm happy to comply. I close my eyes, bracing myself for the worst, and take a sip. It's delicious, rich, and sweet with that vanilla aftertaste.

Wendy smirks at me and goes back to making her breakfast. *Making* is an overstatement since she's merely pouring milk over cereal.

Once she's done, she shakes the box of Cinnamon Toast Crunch at me. "It's not a gourmet breakfast, but would you like some?"

"Yeah, thanks."

She grabs another bowl and fills it with cereal, leaving me to pour the milk.

"What is it we're busy with today?" I ask between mouthfuls.

149

"Shopping," Wendy says. "I need more clothes since my stay got... mmm... octupled? Is that a word?"

"Doubt it," I say. "You want to try the local shops or go to a big department store in Salt Lake City?"

"Mmm." Wendy considers for a second. "I'd say the local stores, but the mall might be more efficient, if less poetic."

I grin as I polish off the last crumbs of food. "Salt Lake City, here we come."

***

The mood during the car journey is a lot more relaxed than I expected. After the initial shock, Wendy seems to have gotten over the hair dye and is back in a cheerful spirit. I'm glad. That ex-boyfriend of hers didn't deserve a single shed tear.

At the mall, we decide to split and meet again for lunch. I watch her study the shopping center map and then pick her direction with certainty. I lean over the big circular display map as well, searching for a bookstore. Second floor, lot B34. I head toward the escalators and after a couple of turns, I find the shop. It's a huge one.

I pass the new releases table. *Eagle Storm,* my latest book that came out this past October, is still front and center: a column of seven copies neatly stacked one on top of the other. I smile and pick up the top hardback.

I check over my shoulders to make sure none of the clerks are looking my way, grab a pen from the inside of my jacket, and sign the first page. I file through the other copies fast, until I've signed all seven.

Job done, I reorder the books and move to the adventure thriller section.

I know I'm acting like an egomaniac, but I immediately search the shelves for the C section. Instead, my eyes fall on the F, where, right in the middle shelf, Darren Floyd's spring release is displayed cover forward. Against my better judgment, I pick up a copy and read the first line.

The last camel died at noon.

Gosh, I hate him. That is a perfect opening line. It conveys setting—some sort of desert, urgency, and it would hook anyone. Normally, I wouldn't have a problem with another writer being brilliant. But Floyd is different. He publicly slandered one of my books after losing a literary prize the year we were both nominees. Ever since then, he's been on my blacklist. It also doesn't help that we're with the same publishing house and our sales figures get constantly compared.

I usually come out on top.

But this year might go differently. If it's true his book is finished and he's trying to steal my holiday slot… he might get the upper hand for once.

The jerk!

Feeling admittedly petty, I flip all his books, making only the spine visible, and rearrange the shelf so that Ken Follett's latest release is cover forward instead. I spend the rest of the morning in the historical fiction section. I open a few novels, read the first chapters, and end up choosing two tomes set in the middle ages. Wendy texts me she's done just as I'm paying.

I take the receipt from the shop assistant, a young man no older than twenty, who keeps squinting his eyes at me, probably wondering where he's seen me before.

For lunch, Wendy and I agree to have Chinese. The restaurant hostess sits us in a booth, thankfully, since Wendy's shopping bags overflow everywhere. She must have a million of them, but two catch my eye over the others—the ones striped pastel pink and cream with the black writing, Victoria's Secret, across the front.

I swallow, wondering about their contents. I can't get even a peek, since the top is covered in pink tissue paper, but I can't help but wonder what's inside. White cotton or lace? Something stripy like the bags?

"Are you all right?" Wendy asks.

I look up and my jaw dangles even further. Now that she's removed her jacket, I notice that she's changed sweaters. The new one is pink and fuzzy and matches her hair.

"You-you've changed sweaters," I blab like an idiot.

Wendy looks down at herself and smiles. "Oh, yes, I couldn't resist. This was just too cute not to wear straight away. Do you like it?"

She looks like cotton candy, and I'm the kid whose parents said he can't have any.

"Yes."

A server arrives, a young woman with long blonde hair highlighted with purple, heavy black liner around her eyes, and a nose piercing. She takes one look at Wendy's hair and gasps. "Your hair…"

Wendy winces. "I know—"

"It's the sickest color I've ever seen. Where did you have it done?"

Wendy seems too stunned to reply, so I offer, "Park City, the hair salon right on Main Street."

"Cool, I'll have to check it out." Then switching gears completely, the young woman's tone becomes mechanical as she asks, "Can I get you started with anything to drink today?"

Once the server is gone with our drink orders, Wendy stares at me with a grim pout. "Don't look so smug. Just because Avril Lavigne liked my hairstyle, it doesn't mean it's cool."

I grin. "Because it's *super* cool, and I think it's growing on you, too."

Wendy frown-smiles at me and goes back to checking her menu.

She orders springs rolls and chicken lo mein, and I get roast pork chop suey and sticky rice in lotus leaf dim sums.

The food arrives fast and, once Wendy has gotten a few bites down, I ask her about the breakup. I want to make sure she's really okay, and that the comeback to life is permanent. "If you don't want to talk about it, it's fine," I add, because I also don't want to push her. Or make her sad again now that she's finally smiling again.

"No." She shrugs. "It's no big deal. There isn't much to it, really. I'm not heartbroken. I didn't lose the love of my life."

I stab a piece of pork. "Why did it bring you so down then?"

Wendy pushes a few vegetables around her plate. "I guess it was two things…"

I give her space to talk in her own time.

After a few bits of silence, she adds, "The first reason is mainly that in all my previous failed relationships I've felt so… forgettable."

I choke on a sip of Coke. Of all the adjectives I'd choose for Wendy, *forgettable* never made the list. "Why would you say that?"

"Brandon broke up with me over the phone after almost two years together like it was nothing."

"But you said you're not heartbroken. Maybe you simply weren't right for each other. He just called it first."

"Yeah, but why doesn't anyone ever fall hard for me?" Wendy looks at me from under her long lashes. "You know, the kind of love that if it ever ended, it would make him want to disappear off the face of the earth and retire to a cabin in the woods to be alone forever."

I swallow, *hard.* "I can't say even that kind of love is all upsides."

"But at least it meant something."

"Still, if you're looking for that kind of love story, it seems to me you were wasting your time with your ex, and I still don't understand why you were so invested in that relationship."

Wendy lowers her gaze and starts to play again with the food on her plate. "That brings us to the second reason I was so down…"

I wait for her to tell me what it was.

"My dad."

I did not see this one coming. "Your dad?"

"Yeah, I feel like I've let him down with another breakup."

"How? Why would you say something like that?"

"Before passing, he'd been sick for a long time. The last two Christmases before this one, we've spent them at the hospital with him. By the second year, he knew he was going, and I knew that, of all his kids, I'm the one he worried about the most."

"Why? Did he say something to you?"

"No, he didn't have to. I mean, in the past, yes." She takes a sip of water. "He was very vocal about the guys I dated in college."

I raise an eyebrow in a silent question.

"Artistry types who thought that to be a genuine artist you had to be penniless…"

I chuckle. "I'm pretty sure you can write excellent prose and still make a good living out of it."

"Agreed, I never aspired to be a starving artist. I love my work, yes, but I don't feel the least guilty about selling it." She waves a hand in the air dismissively. "Anyway, Dad was so happy when I told him I was dating an investment banker. And Brandon will also be the last of my boyfriends he met. I know it might seem silly, but the idea of spending the rest of my life with someone Dad approved of made me feel closer to him even after he left us."

Her words stun me.

So much that I don't realize how long I keep silent, until she prompts, "Have I shocked you?"

"No," I say. "You're the first person I met who understands." At her puzzled expression, I explain. "My mom, she's been gone a few years now, but she knew Cassie, my ex, and loved her. Whenever I think about a future with someone else, I always can't help thinking how they'll never get to know my mom and vice versa."

"You want to talk about the divorce?"

"Nope," I backpedal faster than an Olympic champion.

"What?" Wendy throws a still-wrapped fortune cookie at me. "I just poured my heart out to you and you're giving me nothing?"

"I never said I'd open up in return."

"That was implicit."

"Nah, never assume."

Even with the heavy topics we've been discussing, lunch is fun, easy, cozy. If this were a first date, I would've really enjoyed myself. Except it's not a first date. Wendy probably isn't ready to date anyone at this stage, let alone someone with as much baggage as me. In fact, when I offer to pay, she insists on splitting the bill.

We each sign our receipt and leave the restaurant, heading for the mall's exit. As we walk, a lot of heads turn Wendy's way, mostly women, and a few even stop us to compliment her on her fantastic hair color.

I smirk. "So, it wasn't just Avril Lavigne…"

"Oh, shut up, even if people like it, it doesn't mean *I* do."

"All right, Captain Pook, keep denying all you want."

"Pook?"

"I've joined Pink and Hook… Pook."

Wendy shakes her head, but she smiles. "I don't know what's worse, your taste in hair dyes or nicknames."

I shrug. "Pinkylocks didn't sound right."

***

At home, Wendy refuses to let me help her carry all her ten thousand bags into the house, then she promptly gets tangled on the threshold, trips, and drops a few, spilling the contents all over the hardwood floor.

Given my luck, the Victoria's Secret bags are among the capsized ones. I stare in captured horror as the spilled lingerie pools on the floor. The contrast between the dark wooden planks and mostly white and pink garments is stark. My eyes travel avidly over the lacy, frilly, and shiny fabrics.

Damn.

My earlier curiosity is satisfied, but now I have to deal with the consequences: imagining Wendy in each and every single one of those items.

Thankfully, she makes a quick job of scooping up everything from the floor and unceremoniously throwing it back in the bags.

Last, I gape in horror as she picks up a white satin slip with a see-through lacy bustier.

She catches me staring and asks, "Something wrong with you?"

"What is that?"

Wendy lifts the garment and presses it against her body. "New PJs, you like?"

"What happened to the flannel ones?"

"The attic is sweltering hot compared with our old room downstairs, and the comforter is so much heavier. I've been sleeping in my underwear for days…"

Kill.

Me.

Now.

Twenty-eight

Riven

The next day, I wake up bright and early, rested and ready for my morning routine: shower, coffee, breakfast, write a few thousand words while my brain is fresh, quick break, more coffee, more writing.

It should be just me for a few hours. Except for yesterday, I don't expect Wendy to suddenly become a morning person. She probably wrote until the wee hours of the night and won't get up until noon or something. I don't know how she does it. For me, it's the opposite. I love to write first thing in the morning, while in the evening, my brain goes all fuzzy. I could never follow her schedule.

I hop off the bed and move into the attached bathroom to brush my teeth. I push a dollop of toothpaste on the brush and bring it to my mouth, but the moment the paste comes in contact with my teeth and tongue, I gag and spit.

This isn't toothpaste, it's… *mayonnaise!*

I open the faucet to rinse the awful taste, but no water comes out. I try and retry, desperate to get the tart, salty flavor out of my mouth. But nothing. I bend underneath the sink and discover the water valve has been closed. When I turn it the opposite way, water finally spurts out the faucet. I put my mouth directly under the jet and spit a few times until the taste is gone. Then I stare at myself in the mirror, perplexed.

What the hell is mayonnaise doing in the bathroom? Did I misplace the tubes? I check but, nu-uh, it says Colgate. I squeeze, and more mayo comes out. This was deliberate.

Wendy.

The name flashes in my mind with the sureness of fire. This is her revenge for the pink hair. Despite myself, I smile. Captain Pook got me. I open the faucet again and wipe the spilled mayo from the sink.

When I go to grab the soap bar to wash my hands, I turn it and rub it, but it doesn't lather.

She's broken my soap, too.

How did she do it?

I sit on the toilet to study the faulty soap bar, but the moment my butt hits the closed lid, I shoot back up as a volley of popping sounds fills the room.

What the hell?

I lift the toilet seat and find it rimmed with bubble wrap.

Wendy again!

Wary, and with my hands still sticky with mayo, I approach the shower. Gingerly, I unscrew the shower cap. I wouldn't put it past her to booby-trap the inside with ink or something stinky, but I find nothing. I re-screw the cap in place and try the faucet. Water flows with no glitches and soon turns warm. Okay, it might be safe to shower.

I remove my PJs and step in. Everything goes according to plan until I try to squeeze shampoo in my hands. No product comes out of the bottle. I weigh it in my hands, the bottle is heavy, it should be full. I squeeze again, but nothing gives. Frustrated, I loosen the lid and shake the bottle to see if any liquid would come out. I lift it over my head and study the weird phenomenon. It looks like an invisible barrier is keeping the shampoo inside the bottle. I squint my eyes—oh, for hell's sake. Wendy has bandaged the neck of the bottle with food wrap.

And she's made a thousand loops. The film is slippery and takes forever to pull off, by which time, I'm wet, shivery, and half-frozen to death. I turn the water scorching hot to recover and finally clean myself. I've wasted so much time in the bathroom, my first writing sprint of the day is lost.

Wrapped in a towel, I step back into my room to get some clean underwear. But when I open the drawer, instead of my crisp, white cotton boxer briefs, I find an array of colored underpants. One has a light-blue background with yellow rubber ducks all over it, another is green with bananas printed across, there's a black pair with Christmas lights crisscrossing all over, and a red-and-blue one with a gigantic Superman S on the crotch area. I open my other drawers, but I can't find my real underwear anywhere. The only option left is to pick one of the pairs Wendy kindly selected for me. Each option is equally hideous, but I go for the banana print.

The socks drawer has suffered the same treatment as the underwear one and has been filled with red-and-white striped elf socks. All pairs are the same, so this time I don't have a choice.

She must've bought all of this yesterday at the mall. That's probably why she didn't want me to carry her bags. But when did she sneak into my room to set it up?

The rest of my closet has mercifully been spared, meaning I can finish getting dressed in regular clothes.

In the landing, I pause to check if any noises come from upstairs or downstairs, but both floors are eerily silent. Captain Prank must still be sleeping. Downstairs, I make coffee and power up my computer. I could still try to jot down a few sentences before my stomach protests for its food ration. I take a sip of coffee and choke on it as my screen powers up.

It's cracked!

Wendy has destroyed my laptop.

Oh my gosh, is my manuscript still intact? Accessible?

I have no other copies. Why didn't I listen to Carmen when she urged me to back up my work in the cloud?

I jerk the mouse around, trying to see between the cracks if any of my files are salvageable, but the cursor doesn't budge.

Did she break the mouse, too?

Or is the computer so damaged it doesn't receive signals anymore?

I try the built-in mouse pad and this time the pointer follows my movements. I double-click on the WIP file on my desktop and the draft of my book magically opens, black ink on a pristine white background. No cracks.

I minimize the window and the cracks are back; I maximize it again and the screen is back in one piece. Comprehension dawns on me: she didn't destroy my laptop; she only changed the desktop image. The relief at not having lost all my work of the past few months is so immense, I'm not even mad at Wendy.

I wait for a few heartbeats for my pulse to go back to normal, and then pull up the chapter where I left off yesterday. Instinctively, I grab the mouse to move the cursor to the final sentence, but the gadget is still unresponsive.

But if the computer isn't broken, maybe she just turned it off. I flip it upside down and find a Post-it taped over the back, making it effectively impossible for the sensor light to work. On the piece of paper, she's drawn an evil-looking smiley face.

Okay, Pook, you got me time and time again. I seriously hope the pranks are over, though.

Two hours later, at eleven o'clock, Wendy saunters down the stairs, her lips pressed in a hardly contained smirk.

"Morning," she says innocently. "How's your day going?"

I look up from the screen to meet her mischievous blue eye, the one not underneath the patch. "Without a hitch," I say, beaming at her. I won't give her the satisfaction.

Her suppressed grin breaks into a full smile. "Happy to hear. Want some coffee? I'm making a fresh pot."

I try to keep my focus on my laptop—I was in the middle of writing a great scene—as I half-distractedly reply, "Yeah, sure, thanks."

I tune out the noises Wendy's making in the background and keep typing.

When she hands me a steaming mug of coffee five minutes later, I accept it absent-mindedly and take a sip without thinking. That's when my tongue catches fire. I spit and sputter and, for the second time today, get up to put my mouth right underneath the faucet to rinse the sting away.

It takes a while.

When I feel like I'm able to talk again, I turn to glare at Wendy. She lured me into a sense of false security yesterday by offering me untainted coffee, but she was only biding her time.

The coffee poisoner is casually leaning her elbows on the counter, cuddling an uncontaminated cup. "Something the matter?"

"I thought we were past you poisoning my coffee!"

Wendy twirls a lock of pink hair around her finger. "I only said no more salt."

"What did you use this time?"

"Chili powder." She shrugs. "Gotta keep things fresh, Clark."

"I actually preferred the salt."

"I can oblige you any time."

"Are the pranks over?" I sigh. "You got me, okay? You're vindicated."

With a lazy finger, she traces the rim of her mug. "Am I? I'm not sure… maybe when you least expect it, another trap will snare you." She makes a snatching sound.

"Please, what do I have to do for us to call it even?"

Wendy studies me for a long time before saying, "Just answer one question." She takes a sip of her coffee and eyes me over the rim of the mug mischievously. "Which one of the boxer briefs are you wearing?"

Twenty-nine

Wendy

In the early afternoon after Prank Day, I catch Riven sneaking around the house with a suspicious air about him. Acting all shifty, he grabs the car keys from the cabinet next to the door and puts on his parka.

"I'm going into town," he says, not looking me directly in the eyes. "Need anything?"

Mmm, averted gaze, no invitation to come along. Something is up. He *always* asks me to tag along when he rides into town.

"No, the fridge is full," I say, "and I'm all shopped out for a while. How come you're going?"

Finally looking at me, he says. "I need to buy new underwear."

Sassy answer, but probably an excuse. Something is definitely off.

I could call his bluff, say that I want to go, too, and see how he reacts. Would he come up with another excuse or point-blank tell me no? At least he'd have to admit he doesn't want company. Why? I hope he isn't planning a retaliation for yesterday. Everything I did to him was warranted; I still have the pink hair to prove it.

But, my curiosity aside, I've tortured the guy enough for a while, and he wouldn't be so foolish as to try anything unless he wants pepper in his coffee next. Whatever it is, Riven has a right to his privacy. So, I follow his lead. "Really? What's wrong with yours?"

"The Grinch stole it," he says, putting on a beanie and slinging his feet into his unlaced boots.

Gosh, there's something about men in washed-out jeans and unlaced boots that is just too sexy. *This* man in particular.

"I'll be back in a couple of hours," he adds.

"Yeesh, you must be really picky."

"Picky?"

"Yeah, if it's going to take you that long to buy all-white cotton briefs, do you discriminate on thread count?"

"Bye, Wendy." Riven doesn't take the bait and is out of the door.

Oh, well, curiosity killed the cat, not the playwright.

Alone at the dinner table, I open my laptop and start revising the first act of *Starcrossed,* the new play I've been working on.

Half an hour later, I'm re-writing a line for the thousandth time when the doorbell rings.

Is Riven back already? Did he lose his keys?

Nope. Not him.

When I answer the door, I find a tall man with longish, unkempt blonde hair and a squared, stubble-covered jaw on the other side. The stranger's eyes are hidden behind a pair of fluorescent-orange mirrored sunglasses, and he's wearing the parka equivalent of a Hawaiian shirt. He has a dark-blue duffel bag slung over his shoulder.

"You're not Riven," I say.

He tilts his head to the side, giving me an appraising look, then smirks. "Neither are you. I take it he's not home?"

"No, he went into town. Allegedly, to buy new underwear, but I highly suspect that wasn't the real reason."

"Well, good thing I caught you home then. Can I come in? I'm kinda freezing my arse out here."

Without waiting for an answer, the stranger sidesteps me and walks into the house as if he owned it.

Next, the uninvited guest has the nerve to ask, "Who are you, by the way? I didn't catch your name."

"Excuse me?" I cross my arms over my chest. "You're walking into my house, tell *me* who *you* are."

The guy turns back to me. "*Your* house?"

"I'm paying half the rent."

The man removes his sunglasses and I'm transfixed by his intriguing light-blue eyes. "Ah, interesting development," he says. "I'm Danny, Riven's best friend since our moms had to powder our chubby bottoms."

I could've done without the imagery. "Wendy," I say, purposely withholding the "nice to meet you" part. I'm still holding judgment on that.

"Wendy," he repeats, as if testing out the name. "I'm going to need more details. Nice eye patch, by the way." Danny winks at me, then removes his silly jacket, discards it on the couch with his bag, and goes to open the fridge. "I'm starving, I skipped lunch."

"Please help yourself to whatever you'd like," I say, not sure he'll get my sarcasm. "And we have a no-shoes-in-the-house policy."

"Oh, right, sorry." He pauses his perusal of the fridge to kick off his boots and scatter them on the floor. Mess accomplished, Danny resumes his search. "Do you have any burgers?"

"No."

"Aw, well, at least you got bubbly." He takes a bottle of champagne out of the fridge and then scavenges the cupboards.

"Ah, perfect." Danny finds a bag of chips and empties it into a bowl. Then he grabs two flutes out of a cabinet. "Joining me?"

"Isn't it too early to drink?"

Riven's best friend shrugs. "It's always five o'clock somewhere in the world."

I shrug in return. The guy has a point. I sit on a stool opposite to him and accept the glass he offers me.

"Happy New Year." He clinks his glass with mine. "It's been only a few days. I can still toast to the new year, right?"

"Totally," I agree and take a sip.

"Wendy, dear mysterious Wendy, how come you're Riven's new roommate and I've never heard about you?"

"It's a long story." I grab a chip, with a thrill of mischief and satisfaction at the number of good-dieting rules I'm breaking right now, between the chips and the alcohol. "I don't know if Riven told you about the Christmas double-booking disaster?"

Danny nods.

"Well, my family and his got stuck together for the week and—"

"Wait, wait… you're the hottie from New York? The one he shared a bedroom with? I thought you were a blonde."

I toss my hair behind my back. "That's an even longer story." Then his earlier words register. Did he say *hottie?* Is that how Riven describes me to his friends?

I'm about to ask, when Danny surprises me by rounding the table and pulling me into a bear hug. Guess this guy isn't big on personal boundaries.

"Thank you, thank you," he says. "You resuscitated his Bangaloo. I thought it was dead forever… I'd lost all hope until you came along."

"His Bangaloo?" I repeat. "What's a Bangaloo?"

Danny lets me go. "It doesn't matter. All that matters is that Riven's is alive again." He grabs his glass and clinks it into mine again. "I thought you were going home by the end of the week. How come you're still here?"

I point at my eye. "That's where the eye patch and pink hair come into play."

Denny smiles devilishly. "Tell me everything."

Thirty

Riven

Forty-five minutes earlier

I cross the yard, checking instinctively for canine-like footprints in the snow, but the blanketing is pristine. Apparently, the old wolf didn't visit us last night. Reports of attacks keep surfacing whenever I talk to someone in town, but at least, they haven't been on humans anymore, mostly livestock and a few unfortunate household pets.

That's good news. The bad news is that last night it snowed pretty heavily, and now I'll have to clear a path out before I can drive down the driveway. I drop my laptop bag into the car—I smuggled it out of the house while Wendy wasn't watching—and go to the shed to fetch the snowblower. Twenty minutes later, I've carved a passage large enough for the Jeep. Only now, I'm sweaty, tired, and if I don't hurry, I'm also going to be late.

Luckily, in town, I find a parking spot right on Main Street. As I cross the road to head to my favorite coffee shop, a young man in his mid-twenties, I'd guess, approaches me with a pamphlet.

"Join us in the fight against unnecessary killings," he says as he thrusts the flyer into my hand.

I look at the printout. Green and brown are the dominant colors and the message is mostly about wildlife preservation. "What's this about?"

"The local authorities have promised a reward for the killing of a wolf that's been attacking livestock. We're trying to prevent a pointless slaughter. If you spot the wolf, call the number at the bottom,"—he points at the pamphlet—"and one of our teams will be sent out for a rescue mission."

"What are you going to do with the animal? It attacked two men, isn't it a dangerous beast?"

The activist shakes his head. "Only an old, hungry animal. We believe that with the proper care, he can live his last days in peace in a wildlife rehabilitation center."

I thank him, pocket the pamphlet, and excuse myself.

Inside the coffee shop, only one customer is waiting before me. When my turn comes, I order, and soon after, collect my latte. I pick the table farthest in the back. The view isn't the best from here, but it's the most private spot in the café. With a whole four minutes to spare before my call with my lawyer, I fire up my laptop and put on headphones—results!

I enjoy my sweet, unspiced, unsalted latte waiting for Martha, my attorney, to get online. I could've taken the call at home, shut in my room, or hidden in the basement, or in one of the other free rooms. But I didn't want to discuss divorce proceedings while in the same house with Wendy. It's totally irrational and doesn't make much sense. I've nothing to hide or to be ashamed of. Even so, I want to keep Wendy and the divorce on two separate planes.

Martha calls me at three-thirty on the dot, precise almost to the second. Her face appears on-screen—tan skin, a curtain of black hair, and an expression that means business.

"Hey, Martha, how's it going?" I greet her.

"I'm going to be honest, Riven, things aren't looking up in the settlement." Guess we're skipping pleasantries and getting right to the point. "My firm has received Cassie's requests and they're beyond absurd."

"Okay," I say, grimly. "Hit me."

"She wants the house," Martha says matter-of-factly. "We expected that. But she also claims a right to half of all your liquid assets—"

"What?" I blurt. "Without discounting the house value first?"

"Precisely my point, and—this might sting—she also claims she's entitled to a fifty percent share of present and future royalties for the books you've written while still married to her."

I close my eyes and massage my temples. "On what grounds?"

"Apparently that you named her as your muse in your acknowledgments saying you wouldn't have been able to write such compelling stories without her by your side."

"That's preposterous!" I slam a fist on the table; then, seeing how more than a few heads turn my way, I lower my voice. "And a dedication gives her legal grounds to carry out that request?"

"Cassie's lawyers are being creative, but we can't exclude anything at this point. I just received their requests this morning. I need to make sure there's no precedent before I give you a definitive answer. How do you prefer me to proceed with the rest?"

"She can have the house. I don't want it. But the value needs to be discounted from the liquid assets."

"How hard do you want me to push?"

I consider for a second. The temptation to be petty or vindictive is strong, but I honestly don't think that "winning" the divorce settlement would make me feel any better.

"I wish for the settlement to be fair, Martha, for both parties."

"Okay." Martha shakes her head, while still annotating my requests.

"You think I'm being a pushover?"

Martha looks up at me. "Given the attitude your soon-to-be ex-wife has shown, what I think is that you've always been too good a man for her." She sighs. "Divorce proceedings won't change that. But I'll be damned if I don't make sure you won't be taken advantage of. I'll try to broker the fairest deal possible."

"Thank you, Martha."

"It's my job. And you're a friend, anyway." She waves me off, then picks up the stack of papers in front of her, tidying it. "Can I assume it's a hard no on the royalties?"

My jaw tenses. I still can't believe Cassie would try to claim ownership of my work. "Yes, I wrote those books alone. She has no rights to them."

I won't let my ex walk away with my heart, my house, and my *dignity*.

***

On the journey home, I can't help but feel a wave of bitter anger at the way my marriage is ending. Not that I expected the divorce to be pretty. But, yeah, I still hoped Cassie would at least act like a decent human being, not a money-grabbing, fame-seeking leech.

Wendy is bound to notice my bad mood—and ask questions. I've never had the best poker face. For the first time since she came into my life, I wish I wasn't sharing a house with her.

But, if I'm marginally prepared to deal with her, what I'm most definitely not equipped to cope with is the sight that awaits me when I open the front door: Wendy and Danny, seated at the kitchen island drinking champagne and eating chips out of a bowl.

I have to blink twice, then thrice to reconcile what I'm seeing with what is possible. Am I hallucinating?

But then Danny's booming laugh cracks through the air, and I realize that he's real. I remember his promise to come visit in January. Guess his *"I'll text you when I book my flight"* really translated to *"I'll show up on your doorstep whenever I feel like it and help myself to all your good wine."*

They haven't noticed me coming into the house, so I take a moment to observe them as I quietly remove my jacket, scarf, and boots. They seem to get along. Wendy is smiling and talking, cheeks pink from the wine, I assume, as she pops another chip into her mouth. And, Danny, he's the usual daredevil. Rogue, fun, and also a ladies' man, unfortunately. I hope they won't like each other *too* much.

I hide the computer bag in the coat closet and step into the living room. "Hey," I say. "Do my eyes deceive me or is that really my best friend drinking my champagne and stealing my chips?"

"Ooooh," Danny hollers. "Riven, my man."

He grabs a flute, fills it with bubbly, and comes to offer it to me after crushing me into a bear hug. "You're finally home."

"Did you miss me?" I ask, taking the glass.

"Not really," Danny smirks, gesturing toward the kitchen island. "The wonderful Miss Nichols was catching me up on the latest developments."

I cock my head towards Wendy. "Only good things, I hope?"

She takes a sip of wine and eyes me suspiciously. "Has the Grinch also stolen all the underwear in town?" she asks.

Gosh, that woman is like a dog with a bone. "No, Pook, I didn't go into town to buy underwear."

"You don't say." Wendy smirks, satisfied at my admission.

Danny pats me on the shoulder. "I hope you were up to no good."

Now that the call is behind me, I don't see the point in hiding it. Also, champagne and chips may not be such a bad idea to turn a lousy day around. As unexpected as my best friend's visit is, I'm glad Danny's here.

I take a long sip of champagne before confessing. "Actually," still, as I talk, I avoid Wendy's gaze. "I had a call with my divorce lawyer."

I finally stare up at Wendy and she looks mortified. "Riven, I'm so sorry, I had no idea…"

"Nah, nah, nah," Danny interjects. "We're not going to throw a pity party now, are we? Wendy got dumped, you're getting a divorce, I got my heart broken—"

"Wait, what?" I say, shocked. "I didn't even know you were dating someone? You never date." If there's a hit-and-run version of romantic entanglements, Danny is its master.

"I made an exception," he says, mock-grave or perhaps real-grave. "Clearly a mistake I won't repeat. But that's beside the point because now, we're going to celebrate the new year together, have fun, and flip a gigantic screw-you finger at all our exes." He raises his flute in a toast.

I clink my glass into his. "Cheers to that."

"Cheers," Wendy repeats.

We all drink.

"I need more wine," I say, eyeing the half-empty bottle and refilling my glass. "And more chips."

We toast to the new year.

To new beginnings.

To pink hair.

To banana underwear.

And then I lose count.

"What time is it?" Wendy asks after a while.

I have to squint at my watch twice before properly reading the time. "Almost six."

"Shouldn't we get something to eat?" Wendy asks. "What goes well with champagne, besides chips, I mean."

"Pizza," Danny says.

Wendy and I nod sheepishly in agreement.

"Pizza sounds great," I say.

"Do they deliver up to the woods?" Danny asks.

I grab my phone to call the pizza place, reciting their slogan, "You order, we deliver," I singsong. "The restaurant has a snowcat for when conditions are dire."

Danny nods, impressed. "Guess the good people of Utah have their priorities straight, cheers to them." He raises his glass for the umpteenth toast.

"What's everyone getting?" I ask.

"I'll get a Margherita," Wendy says.

"Pepperoni, double-cheese for me," Danny adds.

"Oh." Wendy scrunches her face. "Now I want the pepperoni, too, and the double cheese."

"Three pepperoni, double-cheese pizzas," I confirm. "How many inches? Fourteen, sixteen, eighteen?"

"Eighteen," Danny says. "Minimum."

"Aren't eighteens too large?" I ask.

"If there're any leftovers, we can eat them at lunch," Wendy says. "Pizza tastes even better the next day."

"Any excuse is good to get out of cooking, eh, Pook?"

I don't mind preparing all our meals, but I also can't help noticing how Wendy has steered clear of the kitchen even in the post-depression days.

"It's for your own safekeeping," Wendy says.

"You mean you can't cook?"

"Nope, I'd have trouble boiling water."

"How do you survive in New York?"

Wendy counts off her fingers. "Frozen dinners, take out, theater vending machines food."

"Atta girl." Danny raises his hand, and they high five.

I shake my head and order three eighteen-inch pepperoni, double-cheese pizzas.

In the end, Wendy doesn't eat half of hers. I just about make it to the middle mark. And Danny is the undisputed champion, he scarfs down three-quarters of his giant pizza. After dinner, the party mood quietens down significantly. Between the alcohol and the food, I'm about ready to pass out even if it isn't nine o'clock yet.

I turn to Danny. "Have you already decided where you're sleeping?"

"I have options?"

"There are two singles upstairs, but one has a full bed."

"And where is Pink sleeping?" he asks Wendy.

"That's none of your concern," I say, coming off more strongly than I intended.

"Uuuh, someone's jealous." He winks at Wendy.

"I'm not jealous. I'm just…"

They stare at me expectantly.

"Drunk, and going to bed." I stand up.

"Party poop," Danny says, but stands up as well, and so does Wendy.

On the upstairs landing, I show Danny where the bathroom and his room are.

"You need anything?" I ask.

"No, man, thanks." He pats his duffel bag. "Everything I need is in here."

I leave him in his room to unpack and find Wendy still waiting for me at the bottom of the attic stairs. "Riven?"

"Yes?"

"What's a Bangaloo?" she asks, rubbing sleep from her eyes. "And why was yours broken?"

"Dead," Danny whispers, poking his head back out of his room. "It was dead."

Thirty-one

Wendy

The next morning, I wake up groaning at my stupidity. Last night, I ate and drank too much. My head is killing me and I feel bloated and gross. I need a three-hour shower. But when I walk into the downstairs bathroom, I find Danny already occupying it.

The shower is going and the room is getting filled with steam, while Danny is the most ridiculous sight wrapped in my fluffy pink towel, with my feathery pink slippers on his feet, and wearing fogged-over sunglasses.

"What are you doing?" I ask.

He turns to me. "Oh, morning, sunshine. I was getting ready to shower, but I forgot my razor in my room so I had to go back." Danny wiggles a foot at me. "Thank you for lending me your slippers."

And my favorite towel, I add in my head.

"How long will you be? I want to shower, too."

Danny raises his sunglasses with one hand, showing bloodshot blue eyes. "Sorry, babe, it's going to take a while." He lowers the sunglasses again.

I cross my arms over my chest. "Do you always shower with your sunglasses on?"

Danny shrugs. "The light was hurting me."

"Well, don't take *too* long."

"Why don't you use Riven's bathroom, Princess, he's out."

I exit the common bathroom and consider Danny's proposition. I shrug and head to Riven's room, crossing the master bedroom to the giant en suite. This bathroom has both a large tub on the left and a shower in the opposite corner. Mmm… which one should I choose?

A long bath beats a long shower any day.

I fill the tub with hot water and bubbles and sink under the delicious warmth. Leaving a trickle of hot water flowing from the faucet to steady the temperature, I relax my head back against the rim.

I don't know how much time I spend in the tub; I might've even fallen asleep at one point. When I wake up, my body feels like it has lost all its bones, and my head has finally stopped throbbing. I drain the water, rise up, and exit the tub on wobbly legs. With a clean white towel wrapped around me and another one around my head, I exit the bathroom.

Then I notice my phone, standing abandoned on the sink, I turn to grab it, and, spinning round again, I smack right into Riven's chest. When I stumble against him, he grabs me by the shoulders to keep me upright.

Once it's obvious I won't break my tailbone on his bathroom tiles, he releases me with a smirk. "Morning."

"Gosh, you can't sneak up on people like that!" I scold and playfully swat him. Then I take a step back, putting space between us. Unfortunately, the move opens up the view to his fully unbuttoned flannel shirt and shiny-with-sweat six-pack. Damn, Mr. Reserved Writer, you're ripped underneath all those nerdy sweaters.

Riven clears his throat, and I'm forced to avert my eyes from the sexy V that leads below his worn-out jeans to stare at his face. Not that it's any better. His dark hair is swept back, sticky with more sweat, and sexy as hell.

"Me sneaking?" he says. "You're the one in my bathroom."

I swallow, mortified that he's caught me staring. I don't want him to think I was drooling, even if I totally was. "Well, your best friend has taken over mine and he said you'd gone out."

Riven smiles. "I was out*side,* chopping some wood."

My lumberjack fantasies skyrocket out of control. I picture him wielding an ax and splitting logs in one clean swoop after the other. In my imagination, he's still wearing the flannel shirt unbuttoned, and his stomach contracts deliciously with every new plunge of the blade. No matter that the outside temperature is in the thirties.

In my mind, I try to reconcile the image of him I'm most used to with this mountain hunk. Riven seated at the table, with a serious half-frown, and glasses on while he types on his laptop vs the sexy wood cutter. He's like the nerdy, smart Clark Kent and muscular, hot Superlumberjack all wrapped into one.

I pretend-sniff the air, wiggling my nose—not for any real reason. I bet even his sweat smells good. "You need a shower."

He beams, rattling me even more. "That was sort of the point of me coming here, but I got detained by a trespasser."

I wrap the towel tighter around my body with the same contempt of a scorned milady in a Regency novel, and, scurrying past him, I say, "I'll get out of your way then."

Riven cocks an eyebrow at me. "Are you going to make me lunch?"

Thirty-two

Riven

Wendy stops and, looking at me over her bare shoulder, she says, "Sure. A wonderful meal will be waiting for you when you get downstairs, sir."

She curtsies.

"I don't know if I should be worried or flattered."

Wendy waves at me. "See you soon." And she's gone.

I get into the bathroom and turn on the tap, hoping Wendy and Danny haven't run through all the hot water. Scratch that, a cold shower is probably what I need after finding Wendy half-naked in my bedroom.

I end up in the middle, with a short, lukewarm shower.

I quickly get dressed and walk downstairs to find the living room smelling surprisingly good. The oven is lit, and the table is laid in a fancier-than-usual fashion.

Danny is already seated at it.

"Mmm," I say. "What's on the menu?"

Wendy, her hair up in a bubble bun, takes something out of the oven—I can't see behind the kitchen island—and sets it on plates, then comes to us with the three dishes in her arms.

She lowers mine first. "Reheated pepperoni, double-cheese pizza for you." She moves on to Danny. "And for you, as well." Then she sits with her own pizza plate in front of her and stares at me defiantly.

I can't help but roar with laughter. "Good move, Pook. But you're not getting out of learning how to cook."

Danny takes a giant bite out of his pizza, moaning. "Best reheated pizza ever," he says between chews.

"So." I look at him, taking the first bite of admittedly exceptional reheated pizza. "You want to tell us more about this mysterious lady who was able to scrape your heart?"

Danny takes a gulp of beer before answering. "You ready to talk about the divorce?"

"Nope."

My best friend shrugs. "Guess we ain't talking then."

Wendy theatrically rolls her eyes, letting out an exasperated, "Men!"

***

After lunch, I hole up in my room to write. I jot down a solid three thousand words and stare away from the screen only when I hear Wendy's footsteps down the stairs. She must've been working on her new play as well and decided to call it a day. I check my laptop's clock, six p.m. Yeah, guess I'm done for today.

I save my work, make sure it syncs with the cloud for double safety—since the faux cracked screen scare I've adopted a new security protocol—and shut the laptop.

Downstairs, Danny is slouched on the couch watching TV and Wendy is leaning against the backrest, cradling a steaming mug in her hands.

"What are you watching?" she asks him.

"A reality show about real estate."

"Oh, are you into real estate?"

"No, I'm into the chicks who sell it," Danny says.

Wendy raises her eyes to the screen. "Yeah, I see your point. And is it fun?"

"Weirdly addictive," Danny says. "I've half a mind to play a drinking game to it."

"Mmm, what would be the rules?"

"Let's see. Every time one of the ladies flips her hair or talks behind someone else's back, we take a shot, double shots if they sell a house."

Wendy chuckles. "I'll get you a beer, but I'm on a detox tonight."

She goes back to the fridge and gets a Coors Light for Danny.

"Make that two," I say.

Wendy jumps at the sound of my voice. "You shouldn't creep up on people like that, sooner or later I'm going to pepper spray you."

"You carry pepper spray around the house?"

"No, but I might start." She hands me the beer.

"Are you sure we can't tempt you to play?" I wiggle the bottle in my hands. "This is basically water."

Wendy narrows her eyes at me. "One episode."

Four hours later we've binge-watched seasons one and two and an array of beer bottles lines the coffee table—turns out these girls talk a lot behind people's backs, constantly flip their hair, and also sell a ton of houses. But between episodes, I've made us a bowl of fettuccine Alfredo to soak the beer, so we're not wasted like last night, not even Wendy who's the lightest weight of the three of us.

"Man," Danny looks up at me. "What do you say we hit the slopes tomorrow? I've gotta bounce in a couple of days, but I'd like to give my legs a stretch first."

"You're leaving already?"

"Yep, gotta leave for Mexico City on the ninth. We film a documentary on Teotihuacán on Monday."

"Yeah, man, I'd love to." I turn to Wendy with an apologetic expression. I know how much she loves to ski, perhaps too much. I stare at the eye patch she'll be allowed to remove in just a few days.

Self-consciously, she touches it. "Don't worry, just because I can't do anything fun doesn't mean you shouldn't."

Danny stands up and bows theatrically. "You shall be missed, Pink, you're a lot of fun." He winks at her, which is the greatest endorsement coming from Danny. Then he turns to me. "I don't know why you ever complained about her."

Wendy's outraged glare turns to me and I scowl at Danny with an unspoken, sarcastic, *thanks, dude.*

"You complained about me?" she asks.

I raise my hands defensively. "Only about your coffee-making skills, I promise." And before she can add anything, I push Danny toward the stairs and follow him up, calling, "Night, Pook."

Thirty-three

Wendy

I spend the next two days basically alone in the house while Riven and Danny go skiing. Then, just as fast as he waltzed into our lives, Danny is gone.

Riven gives him a ride to Salt Lake City airport on Sunday afternoon and comes back just in time for dinner. I didn't want him to have to cook after the drive, so I ordered Chinese and have it ready on the table for us when he arrives.

No matter that I see him every day, the moment he walks into the house and removes his outdoor clothes, my heart jumps in my mouth.

His hair is ruffled from wearing a beanie, messy in a way I'm not used to seeing on him. I want to rake my hands through it and make it even messier. My stomach clenches with yearning.

Unaware of the sexy thoughts floating in my mind, Riven takes in the laid table and takeout boxes, and smiles.

"I ordered you the same things from the other day at the mall," I squeak nervously. "I hope you don't mind."

"Are you kidding? I could eat chop suey and dim sums every day of the week. Thanks for taking care of dinner." He moves to the fridge and opens it. "Glass of wine?"

"Sure," I say, sitting at the table.

It's not the first dinner we've had alone in this house, but for whatever reason, tonight feels different. Date-like, almost.

"How is your play writing going?" Riven asks once he's seated at the table.

"Great, I had two very productive days with you boys out of the house."

"Glad our absence wasn't felt." Riven pops a forkful of vegetables into his mouth and takes a sip of wine before pinning me down with that molten, brown-eyed stare of his. "How did you get into playwriting... it's not the... uh... most common branch of literary artistry."

"You mean you novelists sit at the top of the food chain while all we underlings adore you from below?"

Riven chuckles. "No, I wasn't trying to be a snob. I'm just curious. I never thought of writing anything other than novels, even if, to be fair, LA is all about screenplays. I was wondering if it was the same for you or if something drove you to the theater."

"My dad brought me to the Lunt-Fontanne Theatre when I was ten to watch *Beauty and the Beast*. Two minutes into the show and I'd decided that was what I wanted to do when I grew up."

Riven locks eyes with me and lifts his glass. "To following our dreams."

A flutter spreads in my belly, which the wine only worsens.

The sensation stays with me throughout dinner, which seems to end too quickly.

Once we've cleared the table and loaded the dishwasher, I don't want the night to end. More, I'm desperate for it not to end. I refuse to spend another night in the attic, thinking about Riven in his room below me and how close and distant he is.

An idea strikes me to prolong our evening together. "Hey," I say. "I was thinking of watching another episode or two of the real estate reality show."

And then, putting my hands forward, I add, "With no associated drinking game. You want to watch it with me?"

"Sure," Riven says with a cryptic smile. "But I'm making popcorn."

"After all the food we just ate?"

"You don't have to eat it if you're full."

As if. No one can resist the smell of fresh-made popcorn.

The moment Riven sits at the opposite end of the couch with the steamy bag in his lap, I drift to his side like a bee to honey.

We watch the show sitting side by side, our bodies touching in multiple places. His warmth seeps through my clothes, and I've never felt so good.

At least until his fingers slip through my hair, tickling my forehead.

I look at him curiously as he withdraws his hand.

"A popcorn was stuck between the curls," he says, showing me the puffy ball. Riven throws it in the air and catches it with his mouth.

"That's gross," I complain.

"You're only jealous because you can't catch popcorn with your mouth."

For demonstration, he tosses another one in the air and eats it.

"Oh, yeah?" I grab a handful from the bucket and toss one.

I open my mouth to catch it, but it promptly lands on my nose and bounces off the cushions.

Riven recovers it, throws it, and eats it.

His lips curl into a teasing, sexy smile.

It's too infuriating.

I throw the popcorn still in my hand at him.

His shocked and outraged face is too comical, so I grab more ammunition from the bag and throw it, too.

But Riven's shock wears off quickly. "That's not fair play, Pook."

As he reaches for me, I manage to grab a last handful and throw it before he has my wrists in his hands. He pins me to the couch with my arms above my head, towering over me.

He did it without malice, to stop me from throwing more popcorn at him, but the moment he realizes our new position, the game stops.

His dark gaze makes my heart beat faster and harder, to the point I fear it might crash out of my ribcage.

Riven's grip on my wrists eases, but only so that he can brush his thumbs on the inside in slow circles. The contact sends tendrils of electricity down my body, and I try to bring my arms down, but he doesn't let me. He just keeps gazing at me, lust personified: tall and slender, toned and muscular, but not overly so, the straight nose that wrinkles slightly when he smiles, the right corner of his mouth always upturned in that teasing smile, and his lower lip begging me to bite it.

He's kind, smart, funny, teasing, wicked, considerate, hot. Looks good in a knit sweater and glasses, same as with unbuttoned flannel shirts. Riven Clark and Superlumberjack—a million delicious contradictions all wrapped in a sexy package.

My teeth graze over my lower lip.

In response, that curve of his mouth becomes more pronounced. "What are you thinking about, Pook? You seem preoccupied."

I'm trying hard not to fall into the trap, but like all forbidden things, he has an irresistible allure. Still, I manage a snappy reply. "I was thinking that you weigh a ton, and you should probably go easier on the popcorn next time."

"Oh, really?"

"Really! What are *you* thinking about?" I ask, because what I'm really thinking is how close our mouths are and how little it'd take for us to kiss. And would it really be the worst thing if I lost control? With him. For one night.

"I'm thinking that you should shut up."

Eyes boring into his, I say, "Make me."

His face comes closer until the tips of our noses touch. Riven's chest is gently pressed on mine while our legs are now a single intertwining coil, mine between his. My chest heaves in a labored breath as his scent goes to my head: clean cotton, masculinity, and popcorn.

He lets go of my wrists, trailing his fingers up my palms and lacing them with mine. I remain trapped under him, nailed between his legs, under his chest, my hands clasped in his on the cushion.

My heart is pounding so frantically it's losing beats.

Riven and I, we've been playing a game of poker for a while, but now all the cards are on the table. No more bluffing. I want him, he wants me. It's clear from our heavy, accelerated and short breathing. We can move only in one direction from here. It's inevitable.

Finally, his lips cover that last inch between our mouths that seemed like a mile long until a second ago.

The kiss is sweet as our lips get to know each other. The same lips that have spent weeks making fun of each other, instigating, grumbling, arguing, now look for each other, taste, and discover each other.

My chest surges in response to the kiss. He finally lets go of my hands and I cling to his shoulders, my fingers pushing into his sweater and craving to touch the skin underneath instead. Riven must be on the same quest for bare skin because his hands, blessed with easier access, sneak underneath my sweater and his fingers caress the skin of my lower back. It's the gentlest of touches, but it still burns, sending my senses into overload.

My leg is bent at a weird angle underneath me, but I don't care. I'd lie on hot coals if it meant I could kiss Riven, and from the way my whole body is heating, I might as well be lying on a couch made of flames. Even in the kiss's haze, Riven must notice my slight discomfort, because he rolls us over, our mouths never parting, so that now I'm on top, and with circulation in both legs.

Kissing Riven is transcendental. I hold tight to him as we move together into a new dimension. The real world has disappeared and we exist on a plane made only of us and this desire that is consuming us. Is this what being in love feels like?

My pulse races with the weight of the question and how fast I came to ask it. Or it could be from the way Riven's teeth are brushing my lower lip.

His hands are moving up my back, dangerously close to the clasp of my bra, when a loud crash from the yard makes us pull back. Our eyes meet for an instant. His are wide with surprise and glazed over from the kiss, while a slight frown gives away Riven's annoyance at the interruption. Otherwise, he looks deliciously disheveled. Finally free to roam my hands in his silky hair, I've raked it all directions.

He's so sexy, I have half a mind to ignore the noise and go back to kissing him, when, out of the corner of my eye, I catch a shadow walking past the French windows.

I'm about to scream, but Riven, suddenly serious and

alert, puts a finger over my lips, whispering, "Shhhh."

His touch is searing and sends even more adrenaline flowing down my spine.

Riven straightens up and gently lowers me to the couch.

"You think it's a thief?" I whisper.

"Don't worry," Riven whispers back. "I'm here."

We both refocus our gazes out the windows.

The porch lights are off, and the yard outside is clothed in darkness. The wall-wide French windows that I've always considered as the best feature of the house suddenly seem like a gaping weak spot right in its center.

Inside the house, the lights are off, too, and the only illumination comes from the glow of the TV screen where a "Are you still watching this?" message is gleaming in its center.

We can't see whoever is outside, but can they see us?

Riven stands up, depriving me of his comforting body heat and prompting a shiver to run down my spine. Nothing to do with the hot shudders of just a few minutes ago.

I'm scared something might happen. Plenty of slasher movies are set in cabins deep in the woods for a reason. No one would hear our screams up here.

I reach out to stop him, but Riven smiles at me and whispers, "Don't worry, I'm sure it's nothing. I won't let anyone hurt you."

"Where are you going?"

"To turn on the porch lights."

"But what if they see you?"

"Most thieves don't want to have a confrontation; they might see the lights and flee."

"So, you definitely think there are thieves?"

Jaw tensing, Riven replies, "Only one way to find out."

Thirty-four

Riven

Wendy stands up. "I'm coming with you."

Our faces come level again and I try to ignore how her cheeks are still flushed or her lips swollen from the kissing.

Hundreds of nights alone in this cabin and nothing has ever happened, and the one night I finally get the courage to kiss her, it's home-invasion night.

Must be fate stopping me from making a monumental mistake. I want Wendy. I've been wanting her since the moment she bulldozed her way into my cabin. But I'm not sure I'm what's right for her. She needs certainties, stability, and all I can give her right now are question marks.

Wendy holds my hand and we cross over to the French windows where the light switches are. I flip them all up, and for a moment we stand blinded by the sudden brightness. The entire backyard comes into view, the snow amplifying the light and reflecting it in all directions so that it gives a daylight illusion.

I scan the grounds for any trace of intruders, but don't see any until my eyes meet two glowing yellow pits just at the edge of the woods.

I realize what I'm looking at a second before a bone-chilling howl rips through the night.

Wendy edges closer to me, "Was that a—a wolf? *The* wolf?"

I turn to her, giving her one of my mock-brave smiles. "Good news is, there are no thieves."

Wendy comically hides behind my back, hissing, "Oh, great, because a man-eating beast sounds so much better."

"Come on, wolves don't open doors last I checked. They're not velociraptors."

"And this isn't Jurassic Park, so what do we do now? You have a rifle somewhere?"

"A rifle? To do what? I'm not about to go out into the night hunting for a feral animal who's got a taste for human flesh. And even if I were reckless enough to go out there, I wouldn't know how to shoot. We just need to check the locks." I head toward the kitchen backdoor.

Wendy stays close on my heel, still talking in a low whisper, "Really? I thought that with all the gun fights in your books you were a firearms expert."

That stops me dead in my tracks. I turn back to her and study her for a long time.

"What?" she spats after a while.

"You've read my books?"

Wendy blushes. "Of course I've read your books." Ah, bet the admission cost her. "Everyone has read them."

"But you said nothing, you made it seem like you had barely an idea who I was. Like the only Preacher Jackson knowledge you had was hearsay."

"Well, when we first met, you seemed enough full of yourself not to need an extra boost to your already disproportionately large ego."

"Is that so? Does that mean you liked them?"

"Yes, you're the master of adventure and suspense. Your novels are unputdownable—happy?"

The praise, despite being wrestled out of her, fills me with pride.

"Very," I reply.

193

Wendy rolls her eyes. "Can we take care of the wolf situation now?"

I reckon it's too late at night to call the wildlife association. And since we're in no real danger, it'd be pointless to alert the town marshal. A commando of hunters armed to the teeth in our yard would be far more dangerous than a poor starving animal.

Wendy and I make a round of all the locks in the house, checking both doors and windows. Once every single one is secured, we come back to the living room, awkwardly standing a foot apart. The moment is gone. The perfect atmosphere of before evaporated.

"Do you want to finish the episode or should we just go to bed?" Wendy asks, hugging herself.

I snort, throwing a resentful glare at the stairs, all too aware tonight won't be ending as I would've liked. No matter that I suspect it wasn't the best move, to begin with.

Wendy shifts on her feet, darting a suspicious look at the French windows as if she expected the wolf to crash through at any second. And I, too, am a little scared. Only the thing that terrifies me is that tonight was just a fluke and I won't get to kiss her again.

"Bed, I think," I say. "Are you going to be all right?"

"Yeah, sure, as you said, wolves don't open doors."

Just as she finishes the words, another eerie howl echoes outside.

Wendy is hiding her face in my chest in a fraction of a second.

I wrap my arms around her. "Afraid of the big, bad wolf?"

"Would you think me silly if I said yes?"

I push a lock of silky pink hair behind her ear. "No, I have to admit that old renegade is pretty scary."

"Riven...?"

We are next to the stairs, facing each other.

"Yes?"

"Can I sleep in your bed tonight?" An electric bolt courses through my body before she can finish. "I mean, *only* sleep. I know I'm being irrational, but I'd like to have you close because I'm scared."

The request is so sweet I can't breathe.

I kiss Wendy on the forehead, hugging her to my chest. "Of course," I say. "But please, wear the flannel pajamas or I might go insane."

Her eyes widen and her mouth forms a little surprised O before curling into a secret smile.

I offer her my hand. Wendy looks at it and then at me. Intensely.

And that look tells me a lot of things, everything we can't tell each other. Not yet. Maybe not ever.

And then, she just puts her hand in mine, her smirk turning a little evil as she asks, "Not a fan of Victoria's Secret?"

"Keep being a smart aleck and you're going to sleep alone."

She rises on her toes and kisses me on the cheek. "You wouldn't be so mean."

No, I wouldn't. *Sleeping in the same bed with you will be the best thing I've ever done—and the hardest.*

I smile at her and precede her up the stairs, pulling her after me, until she goes up to her room to change.

She tiptoes back into my room not ten minutes later and scoots under the covers.

And the simplest and most beautiful night of my entire existence begins.

Thirty-five

Wendy

Everything was perfect.

And then that stupid wolf had to crash into the yard and ruin everything with its howling.

But now that I'm in Riven's bed, with him peacefully breathing next to me, his arm wrapped around my waist, I'm not sure if I should be angry at that old beast or grateful.

Riven has been a true gentleman and didn't try anything. He's held me close to make me understand I was safe but in a respectful way. I smile in the dark, thinking how, as long as he's been awake, he's tried to keep a safe distance between us, even while hugging. And how, now that he's sleeping, he's smothering me with his body heat. One leg swung over my thigh, head resting in the nook of my shoulder.

I've never felt safer in my entire life.

I run a finger down his arm, only prompting him to snuggle closer.

"Thank you," I whisper, planting a soft kiss on his temple.

I don't want to sleep. I try to stay awake as long as I can, savoring every second of this new intimacy. But the rhythm of Riven's chest swelling up and down and the warmth of his body soon become too much. My lids turn heavy, my eyes close, and I give in to sleep...

***

I wake up at the first light of dawn and rub my eyes in the semi-darkness. The faint glow of the sunrays barely filters through the windowpane.

I turn sideways seeking Riven, but he's not in bed with me.

The discovery makes me bolt upright. Already considering all the worst possibilities, I search the room with my gaze for him just as he shuffles in from the adjoining bathroom wearing only a towel. I swallow.

Okay, a guy who spends most of his days seated at a desk has no right to look like that.

Our eyes meet and he flashes me a grin. "Morning."

"What time is it?"

Riven comes to the bed and sits next to me, planting a kiss on my forehead. "Stupid early," he says.

He smells like soap and sin. A few droplets of water fall from his hair on my collarbone and I'm relieved when they don't start to sizzle and evaporate instantly, because that's how hot I feel right now. And why did I ask him to only sleep with me last night? I'm a stupid cow.

Riven pulls back and tucks me better under the covers. "Go back to sleep."

"Where are you going?"

"I've dreamt of a perfect scene for my novel and I want to jot it down before it's gone."

I sigh. "I can't fight sudden inspiration, go."

He smirks at me. "Wendy?"

"Yes?"

"I loved last night, and I don't know what the future holds, but would you like to go out on a date with me?"

My belly flutters. "A date?"

"Yeah, I know we're sort of eating dinner together every night, but I want to take you out. Dress up. Wine and dine you properly and kiss you goodnight at the end of the night."

Can't you just kiss me good morning? I want to ask, but I don't. He's being so sweet... and I like him even better for not wanting to rush things, even if waiting will be small torture.

"I'd love to go on a date with you."

The joy and relief on his face would be comical if they weren't so heartwarming. "Tonight?"

"Tonight," I agree.

Riven kisses me on the forehead one last time and, grabbing a change of clothes, goes downstairs. I hide my face under the covers, kicking my feet up and down under the blankets in celebration.

***

When I open my eyes again, the sun is shining high in the sky. Unable to wipe a silly smile from my face, I grab my phone and text Mindy.

> I slept with the hot writer last night

Mindy sends me a head-exploding emoji, followed by a question:

> Was the sex mind-blowing?

198

I don't know, we only slept together

I explain to her the wolf situation and add:

But the kissing was really promising

Next steps?

He's asked me on a date tonight

A date?

Yeah, he said he wants to wine and dine me properly. Like a real gentleman

I've only two pieces of advice

Yeah?

Shave your legs and wear pretty underwear

Do you have a fixation on shaved legs?

I went on a date once, and mine weren't

I still bear the scars

Oh, come on, a little leg hair couldn't have been that bad

No, except that I tried to covertly shave in the guy's bathroom after having too many appletinis

And when I talk about scars, I don't mean emotional either

I mean actual flesh wounds on my legs

I chuckle, shaking my head and clasping the phone to my chest. Mindy is just priceless, but her razor horror stories aren't the reason I can't stop smiling all day.

I haven't felt this giddy... well, if I have to be honest, probably not since my parents gave me the Barbie magical mansion Dreamhouse for Christmas in the second grade.

I get dressed and move one floor up to the attic, funneling the adrenaline of anticipation into my work. I'm so taken I would've skipped lunch if Riven hadn't brought up a club sandwich for me.

After the short break, my fingers fly on the keyboard until I reach a crossroads in the plot. Initially, I'd planned for this play to end without a happily ever after. Something a la Romeo and Juliet where no matter how much the characters love each other; the universe will pull them apart. But the more I write, the more they push me to be together... could I give them a happy ending? Would the story still work? I try to imagine a version of *Titanic* where Leonardo Di Caprio lived.

Nope.

I need to break them apart, but perhaps not today. I'm too loved up to write about heartbreak.

Tiptoeing downstairs, I poke my head over the banister to check the living room. Riven is seated at the main table, writing—glasses on, concentrated frown, pouty lips. There's my Clark Kent.

Conscious of how hard it is to get into the writing flow, I don't want to interrupt him. Even a minor distraction could set his work back by an hour or more before he gets into the "writing zone" again. I backtrack up the stairs and send him a text instead—he always silences his phone when he's writing.

> Using your bathtub

> Didn't want to interrupt your writing

With Mindy's advice fresh in mind, I bring a razor to the tub but before stepping in, I pause in front of the mirror to remove the pink eye patch and bandage underneath. I squint at my reflection, waiting for the usual stab of pain direct light causes my eye, but it doesn't come. My vision is blurred at first, but it quickly comes into focus once my pupil adjusts to being free again.

To make sure I can go without the protection, I check the dates on my calendar. Yep, the doctor cleared me to remove the patch since yesterday. Great!

I throw the white gauze in the bin and stare at the pink patch fondly, whispering, "I'm actually going to miss you."

I spend the rest of the afternoon scrubbing, shaving, and pampering.

When it comes time to change for our night out, I sigh at my open closet. Regretfully, I didn't bring or buy a dress. I never thought I'd need one on a ski trip. Instead, I opt for a pair of skinny jeans and my new fluffy pink sweater. Riven seemed to really like it at the mall. I wish I had high-heeled boots to go with the outfit, but it's probably better I only have my Timberland. With serious heels in this climate, I'd slip on the ice, fall on my bum, and embarrass myself forever.

I style my hair in soft waves and let it loose on my shoulders. And for makeup, I only put some blusher on, as I don't feel comfortable applying anything near my eyes yet.

When I get downstairs, ready to leave, I stop on the last step of the stairs as Riven barrels into the cabin, followed by a drizzle of snow. He shuts the door in a hurry, and when he stares up at me, he freezes.

"Hey," I say.

"Hy—err..." he clears his throat. "You look amazing. And the eye patch is gone!"

"Thanks." I self-consciously pull a lock of hair behind my ear. "It was time to remove it."

Riven smirks. "You looked gorgeous even with the patch on."

"Well, at least now I'll make slightly fewer heads turn in town with only the pink hair." I eye his casual clothes dubiously. "Are you ready to go out or do you need more time to get changed?"

Riven's face falls. "About that... I don't think it's a good idea to go into town in this weather... I went to check the road and it's awful and getting worse by the minute."

I hop off the last step and get closer. "It's okay," I say, "we can stay in..." That might be actually better since dinner right now felt like the longest torment before I could get to the dessert: my Superlumberjack.

"How about we cook instead?" Riven asks, removing his scarf and beanie.

Underneath the hat, his hair is sticking up in all directions and, now that I have more confidence, I can't help but rake my fingers through it, asking, "We?"

"Yep, time for your first cooking lesson, Pook."

Riven grabs my hand, twirls me around in a pirouette, and catches me at the end of the turn. Our chests come in contact, and I tilt my chin up. Riven doesn't need any more incentive to close the distance between us and put his lips on mine.

I want to pull him closer, but his puffy jacket is creating too much of a buffer. I trail my fingers down its front, undoing the buttons and pushing it off his shoulder.

Meanwhile, his hands sneak underneath my sweater, and… they're freezing cold. I squeak and instinctively pull away.

"Your hands are too cold," I explain.

Eyes all intense, Riven grabs me by the hips, lowering his forehead to mine. "Saved by the chilly hands, Pook." He presses a gentle kiss on my temple and pulls back.

He picks up his parka from the floor where I discarded it and hangs it on the rack by the door. Unconsciously, he runs a hand through his hair, still flattened from the beanie. Then he turns and, balancing on one foot in a sort of half-bent tree yoga pose, unlaces his boots. Riven repeats the process with the other boot and for a moment he stands there, faded-out jeans, button-down knit sweater, and unlaced boots.

Lately, unlaced boots have become the sexiest thing in the world. I'm developing a real weakness for them. When Riven kicks them off, it's not like he's removing his pants or something, but I still bite my lower lip and stare up at him, wondering if we can't just skip dinner already.

When our eyes meet, he studies me for a second and cocks his head to the side. "So, what do you want to make for dinner? You look pretty hungry, Pook."

Yep, I reply silently in my head, *just not for food.*

"I'm in the mood for pasta," I reply, only because it's supposedly the easiest, quickest meal to make.

"Any particular sauce?"

"Something simple."

Riven strolls to the kitchen and opens the fridge and a few cabinets. "Why don't we start with the very basics?"

I join him in the kitchen. "What did you have in mind?"

"A simple tomato sauce?"

"Oh, I already know how to make spaghetti marinara."

Riven raises a skeptical eyebrow. "Yeah? What's the recipe?"

"Boil the spaghetti and pour the sauce from the jar on top."

Riven's shoulders shake with laughter. "No, Pook, no shortcuts. We're making the sauce from scratch. Don't look so hopeless," he adds, planting a soft kiss on my neck, "It's really easy."

I shiver, thinking the only thing I'm hopeless about is skipping this damn dinner and getting him into bed.

"Okay," I say. "Walk me through the steps."

Riven moves in front of the sink and rolls up his sleeves to wash his hands. For a moment I get distracted by his lean forearms… these days I get fixated on the weirdest things. Then I get a grip on myself and join him at the sink.

"Soap please?" I say.

He gives me a playful look that makes my stomach flip and, instead of handing me the soap bar, he grabs my hands and brings them under the jet of lukewarm water. In slow circles, he works the soap on my palms, lathering them with soft, thick foam. Then, he drops the bar and intertwines his fingers with mine, working his thumbs on the back of my hands. For something that's supposed to get me cleaner, this hand-washing business feels rather dirty.

The massage is soothing and relaxing. I close my eyes and lean into his body, humming. Until he brings our joined hands back under the water and the magic is over.

I slowly open my eyes. Riven is looking at me, eyes soulful, jaws tense.

"From now on, you're always washing my hands," I say to break the tension.

Riven smirks, but the intensity doesn't leave his gaze as he towels me dry with a kitchen cloth. Too soon, he lets me go and opens the fridge to take out a plastic container of cherry tomatoes, some basil, and garlic.

Like a professional chef, he arranges all the ingredients in a tidy display on a cutting board. "You want to put the water on the stove to boil in the meantime?" he asks. "If it's not too hard."

I bump my hip into his. "Are those your smarty-pants you're wearing?" And bend down to retrieve a pot. I fill it in the sink and set it on the stove. "Tah-dah."

"Take my place," Riven says. "Keep cutting the tomatoes in quarters."

As I man the vegetable station, he takes out a frying pan and, with a flaring gesture, sprinkles the base with olive oil. Then he adds a few peeled garlic cloves.

"Shouldn't we cut them, too?" I ask.

"Not unless you're keen on repelling Count Dracula for the rest of your life. I like to leave them whole. That way the garlic adds to the flavor, but it's easy to discard, saving us from the vampire-chasing breath."

"How many more tomatoes should I cut?" I ask, as the garlic begins to sizzle.

Riven throws an assessing stare at the tomatoes. "Half the box?"

"What now?" I ask when I'm finished.

"Throw everything into the pan."

"Just like that?"

He nods and grabs a pinch of salt from a jar, sprinkling it on the tomatoes as I drop them in the pan.

Riven comes behind me and adjusts the flame under the stove, lowering it slightly. Then he clutches a wooden spoon and hands it to me. "Now we stir."

Even if we aren't touching, the bulk of his body behind me is too close. All-encompassing. I grab the spoon, but don't actually move it. I'm too distracted by the heat emanating from him.

When I let the wooden spoon just lay limp in the pan, Riven gently grabs my wrist and shows me how to stir the sauce in slow circles.

I know how to stir.

But right now, I've lost all mind-body coordination. His presence, his warmth, his smell that not even the steam from the sauce can cover... it's all too much.

I lean into him, molding my back to his front. Riven goes rigid for a second, but next, his free hand lands on my hip, pulling me even closer, wrapping around my waist. I drop the wooden spoon into the pan and tilt my face upward and backward. His lips descend on mine, and we kiss.

The kiss is deep, intense, passionate. But it's not enough. I need more, I want more of him, I need to feel him closer. I turn and wrap my arms around his neck, my fingers sinking into his soft hair as I pull him toward me.

Riven lifts me up and sets me on the kitchen counter, trailing kisses down my neck. I circle my legs behind him and force him closer with the press of my thighs, making sure there's not even an inch of air between our bodies.

I don't know how long the kiss lasts. It could be a minute, it could be an hour before an insistent *beep, beep, beep,* penetrates the haze of our passion.

Riven and I pull back at the same moment, I stare to my left at the blackened content of the pan, which is frizzing while it carbonizes, producing a black, smoky cloud. Riven moves to the side to turn the smoke detector off.

I bite on my swollen lower lip, staring up at Riven from under heavy lashes. "The sauce looks ruined."

"Good," Riven says, dropping the pan in the sink and turning off the stove. "I wasn't hungry anymore."

He scoops me up from the counter as if I weighed nothing, his hands solidly under my bottom as I straddle him.

"Where are we going?" I ask, bumping my forehead into his.

Lips curling up in a lopsided smile that promises heaven and hell, Riven says, "You've been a bad girl, I'm taking you to bed without dinner."

Finally!

Thirty-six

Wendy

The next morning, it takes me a minute to realize why I'm feeling so utterly blissed out. When I do, I throw an arm over to the other side of the bed but find it empty.

I blink awake and take in Riven's bedroom.

Where did he go?

Does he regret last night?

Was he afraid of the morning-after awkwardness?

I'm still rolling through possible worst-case scenarios in my head when he reappears on the threshold with a tray... breakfast in bed.

He's wearing the Superman boxer shorts I bought him— he's earned them—and an unbuttoned flannel shirt. My toes curl under the sheets and the knot of anxiety in my belly unwinds: no awkwardness here.

"Morning," he says, coming over to the bed and placing a kiss on my forehead before dropping the tray on the mattress.

I take in the perfect display of coffee, orange juice, croissants, jam, and butter and raise an eyebrow. "Croissants?" I ask. "Where'd you get them?"

"From my secret frozen stash."

"For when you have a girl up here?"

"No, for when I have a sudden craving and we're snowed in like today. Bad news, Pook, you're stuck inside with me all day."

"Story of my life," I say, smirking.

I stare at the white-hot glare of the sun reflected on the mountain peaks. Any trace of last night's storm is gone, and it looks like it's a glorious, icy day. But I'm happy to enjoy the view all warm from underneath the covers.

"Is the road still blocked?"

"Yep." He taps my nose with a fingertip. "But don't worry, the agency has a snowplowing service… they'll come to free us… eventually!"

"Oh, so you plan to keep me in your bed all day?"

"Now that I finally got you here… hell, yeah."

"What do you mean *finally?*"

"That I've wanted you in my bed since I first laid eyes on you."

The same goes for me, but I still frown at his confession. "What? You acted as if you hated me."

Riven lifts his mug of coffee in a mock toast. "It was a defense mechanism from all the poisoned coffee."

I swat him playfully. "But if you liked me, why didn't you say something sooner?"

He smiles. "First you were spoken for, then you were depressed, then angry at me—"

"You dyed my hair pink!" I protest.

"—and then Danny arrived."

"Oh, I see, so you were just waiting for him to leave."

"To await a pleasure, is itself a pleasure."

"Oh, so would you rather still be waiting?"

"No way."

And he kisses me to show me just how much he's not willing to lose another minute.

And it's a pity really that such an excellent breakfast should go to waste… but, priorities… I'm afraid food didn't make it to the top of the list also today.

Thirty-seven

Wendy

One month later

Being with Riven is as full of delicious contradictions as the man himself. In bed, he's gentle, but strong and manly at the same time.

Physical intimacy was the last barrier between us, and once it got broken—shattered—we jumped from a first date to basically "moving in together" in the span of a night.

We're still getting to know each other, but living like a married couple—in a very deep, can't-get-their-hands-off-each-other honeymoon phase. The days blur in a haze of mornings spent writing, laughing, talking, cooking... and nights spent making love. We settle into a rhythm where days turn into weeks quickly. Maybe we're going too fast, maybe I've yet again jumped into a new relationship before my last one was cold in the ground, but this time it was for all the right reasons.

Like every morning for the past month, I wake up in Riven's bed and reach out my hand to his empty half.

I sigh.

Darn morning person. He got up early to write like every other day. Riven says his manuscript is almost done, but has refused to let me read a preview before it's complete. I'm sure it's going to be genius, same as all his previous books.

Gosh, he's brilliant, gorgeous, kind, considerate, sexy, amazing between the sheets, and he can cook... Other than when he dyes my hair pink without my consent, he's perfect and I lov—lah, lah, lah, lah, lah… I push the L-word out of my head.

Nuh-uh, not going there, not touching that.

On the nightstand, my phone pings with a reminder, and I welcome the distraction. But when I check the notification, my heart sinks in a panic.

My final doctor's appointment is next week.

The reminder makes me realize just *how much* time has passed. In a matter of days, the doctor is going to check my eye and tell me if I'm ready to go home. And then what?

Riven and I have both lived in the moment for the past few weeks, I've never brought up the future and neither has he. Why? I didn't do it because I didn't want to push hard questions on him. He's not even divorced yet. Will he be ready to discuss a future with me?

I stare back at the notification on my screen. Well, I can't hide my head under the bedsheets anymore. *Starcrossed*, my play, is finished—has been for a while. I honestly have been over-revising it in the last week or so. As soon as the doctor clears me for flying, I need to return to New York to submit it to producers.

I put on a fleece robe, ready to go downstairs and have *The Conversation* with Riven when the doorbell rings. Uh, weird, who could that be at nine in the morning? The mailman never comes until mid-morning. From the sounds he makes downstairs, I follow Riven's progress across the living room as he goes to answer the door. The scrape of the chair as he stands up, his muffled footsteps on the hardwood, and the snap of the lock as he opens the door.

Then silence.

An unnatural, loaded pause that seems to last forever until Riven asks, "What are *you* doing here?"

His voice is impersonal, guarded, almost unrecognizable. I shuffle out of bed and tiptoe to the landing.

"Hi," a woman replies. "I know I'm the last person you expected to see, but can we... talk?"

She, on the contrary, sounds hopeful and apologetic. The foolproof realization that this is the voice of his wife hits me even before he says her name. "Cassie..."

It's just a name, but Riven's tone is loaded with so much shared history, it sinks into my heart like a knife.

"Can I just come in?" the ex-wife asks. "It's freezing out here."

She must push her way into the house because next, I hear the door closing.

I sit on top of the stairs, listening in.

"What are you doing here?" Riven asks. "When did you get in?"

"I took a flight yesterday. I'm staying at a hotel in town since I didn't want to ambush you last night."

Ah, I mentally scoff. I wish she had ambushed him last night. She would've been in for quite the surprise. I close my eyes and try to shut out the memory of Riven and me making love on the living room rug in front of the fireplace.

"My lawyer said I shouldn't speak to you directly," Riven's voice cuts through the haze and makes me refocus on the present.

"Talking only through our lawyers... is this what we're reduced to?"

"It's what you made us." His reply comes out evenly, but it's still filled with hurt. And if she can still make him hurt... does it mean he still loves her?

"It doesn't have to be that way, not anymore."

"Why don't I find it odd that the first time you reach out to me after months of radio silence is right after your new fling tossed you aside—I saw the article," he says.

What article? About the actor she cheated on him with? Is the guy dating someone new? And why does Riven know? Was he still stalking his ex online while sleeping with me?

"We broke up a while ago," Cassie says flippantly. "And it was never about him, you know perfectly well the reasons I left and they had no—"

She suddenly stops talking, and I hear heels clacking on the hardwood floors. "Do you have a woman in here?" The words come out filled with venom.

"That's none of your business."

"Oh my gosh, you do. Who is she, *your girlfriend?*" The sneer in Cassie's voice makes my skin crawl.

"She's not my girlfriend," Riven says. "We're roommates."

Ouch. That hurt. That physically hurt. Like a brick hurled at my chest.

"Roommates? Since when do you do roommates?"

"Since it's none of your business."

"Oh, I see. Is this roommate sleeping in her own bed or yours?" Cassie asks tartly.

Riven doesn't reply. There's a long silence… what the heck are they doing? Could I crawl down a few more steps and have a peek?

No, if they spotted me, I'd die of embarrassment. Also, I want to hear what else Riven has to say about me, *about us.* So far, the eavesdropping has been really informative.

"Okay," Cassie says after a long time. "Maybe it's actually better that you've had a side piece for a while."

"And why would that be?"

"Because you've had your little fun, and now that we're even, we can move on."

"Move on to what? We're done, Cassie. Done. You cheated on me, humiliated me, abandoned me. You didn't even have the courtesy to inform me when you filed for divorce. I had to learn it from my attorney! We're never going to be even, not in a million years."

"You're angry, I get it. And I've made mistakes, but are you really going to throw ten years of your life out the window as if they never happened?"

Another long pause. Oh my gosh, what is he going to say? Is he going to take her back? My heart is beating so hard in my chest I'm scared they'll hear the thumping and discover me.

"Cassie," Riven says at last. "I've had nine months to come to terms with the fact that *you* threw away ten years of life together on a whim. Whatever was between us, it's long dead, there's no going back. Ever." His tone is final.

Cassie must hear the resolution, too, because next, she hisses, "Screw you. Screw you and that ho you have upstairs."

Heels clack on the floor and then the front door slams shut.

Thirty-eight

Riven

The glass rattles in the frame as Cassie slams the door. I wait, ears tense, for the sound of tires scrunching over the snow outside. My ex is from Wisconsin, originally, so I'm not worried about her ability to drive on snow. I just want to make sure she's gone for real.

I pace up and down the hall, trying to calm down. My hands have gone clammy and my throat dry. I hate that she still has the power to upset me so much. True, I haven't seen my wife in almost a year, but I thought I'd be indifferent to her by now.

Turns out I'm not.

My gaze travels up the stairs. Is Wendy awake? Did she hear us?

I walk up a few steps and find her sitting on the landing with a crushed expression. Guess that answers my question.

"Wendy."

"Hi, roomie." She waves sarcastically.

I wince. "How much did you hear?"

"The entire conversation. It clarified a few things for me. Like how I'm not your girlfriend and how we're only roommates with benefits, apparently."

"Wendy, come on." I walk up the steps until our eyes are level. "I wasn't about to discuss us with my ex."

"Okay." She stands up. "Discuss *us* with me, then."

"What do you mean?"

Wendy stares down at her phone. "I woke up this morning to an alert for my next doctor appointment. It's next week."

"Okay, what's the matter? I'll drive you like always."

"It's the *last* appointment, Riven. Dr. Curt is probably going to clear me for flying, and then what? What happens to us?"

That can't be right. It can't have been two months already. Sheepishly, I ask. "What day is it?"

Wendy stares at her phone and cringes. She turns the screen toward me. "February fourteen, happy Valentine's Day."

"Sorry," I say. "I hadn't realized."

"Me neither and I don't care about a stupid made-up holiday. I care about the other 364 days of the year. My play is ready, written, over-edited. I've already wasted days on a script that doesn't need more work. As soon as I'm cleared for flying, I must go back to New York to shop it around."

"Okay. The timing and geography are complicated. We obviously can't date like two normal people and see where this goes, but—"

"Timing? Geography?" she doesn't let me finish. "If you talk about the weather next, you're going to officially win the prize for the lousiest breakup ever."

"I'm not breaking up with you."

"Right you aren't, because we've never been together in the first place."

Wendy storms up the stairs to the attic. I follow her and enter her room just as she drags her suitcase across the floor to open it onto the bed.

"What are you doing?"

"Packing."

"Why?"

"The high season is over. If Cassie can find a room in town, so can I."

"I don't want you to leave."

She stops flinging clothes at random into the case and wheels on me. "You want me to stay?"

"Yes."

"For how long?" she hisses. "A week, a month? Because it sure as hell isn't forever."

She's asking me for a commitment I'm not sure I can give. Not with my divorce still unsettled. Not with the way Cassie made me cold sweat less than twenty minutes ago. My head and my heart aren't clear enough to make such an important decision. I could lie and say that I'm ready, but I'd be gambling with Wendy's happiness alongside my own. And while I'd be willing to take that risk for myself, I can't do this to her. I care too much.

I tell her the truth. "I can't give you that kind of commitment right now. I'm not ready."

Wendy's features soften, turning more sad than angry. "And I can't settle for anything less."

A battle rages in my chest. Part of me wants to go to her, tell her that, of course I want to spend the rest of my life with her. But the rational part prevails once more. Wendy Nichols is a woman that deserves one hundred percent, and Cassie's visit today proved I'm not free to move on yet. I need to settle my past before I can look at my future.

I give Wendy a stiff nod. "I'll let you finish packing."

Her lower lip quivers and I flee the room. If I saw her cry now, I'd make promises I'm not sure I can keep. I go wait for her downstairs on the couch, elbows on my knees. Head in my hands.

When I hear her drag the suitcase down the stairs, I try to help her, but she makes a point of taking it down on her own.

"Do you know where you're staying?"

"Yeah," she says in a small voice. "I've called Kelly Anne. She's set me up with a week's rental in Salt Lake City, closer to the hospital and the airport."

I nod. "I'll give you a ride."

"You don't have to; I can call a cab."

"No, I'll drive you."

We put our coats on in silence. I grab the car keys and exit the front door, only to stop dead in my tracks. Across the yard, a massive black wolf is staring directly at me.

I fling my arms out to prevent Wendy from walking past me. "Go back inside," I whisper.

The wolf sets a paw forward, his eyes never leaving mine.

"Riven, please, I just want to go."

Wendy struggles to move past me, but I keep blocking her. The moment I break eye contact, the beast is going to pounce, I can feel it in my bones. In a split second, I throw Wendy's suitcase to the side, turn, and shove her back into the house, slamming the door shut behind us.

"What are you doing?" Wendy asks.

"The wolf," I say. "It's in the yard."

She crosses the living room to the French windows. "Oh my gosh, it's massive. But also, so thin. What's he doing out in the day?"

"He must be desperate for food," I say, whipping out my phone.

"Who are you calling?" Wendy asks. "You can't call the marshal, they'll kill him. Look at him, he's starving."

"I'm not calling the marshal. I'm calling the environmentalist association that's filling the town with rescue pamphlets."

The conversation is brief, and the moment I hang up, Wendy asks, "What did they say?"

"To throw a lot of food out the window to keep him nearby. It'll take them an hour to send a team."

"What do they plan to do?"

"Shoot him with tranquilizers and bring him to an animal rescue center where once he's well-fed, they hope he'll lose his aggression toward men."

I open the fridge and grab a few sausages and a steak.

"Stay back," I say. "I'm going to throw these out on the porch."

"You can't seriously mean to go outside."

I look out the French doors. "The wolf's not there now, but he'll come back once he smells the meat. I'll keep the door open for just a second."

Once I come back inside, Wendy is still wearing her coat, arms wrapped around her waist in a self- hug.

I go to her. "Are you scared?"

Teary eyes meet mine. "Yes, but not of the wolf."

I hug her, taking in her smell, her softness, her warmth. "I'm sorry," I whisper in her ear.

"I know," she whispers back, then she looks up at me. "Riven?"

"Yes?"

"Please make love to me one last time."

Thirty-nine

Wendy

Nine months later

Starcrossed is happening. As of ten minutes ago, the agreement is in black and white. Casting will start next week, then rehearsals, and, next September, the debut. As I walk the streets of New York City, I should feel ecstatic. Instead, I stare at the tall buildings and sparkly shopping windows with total emptiness. This city that used to provide me with endless inspiration, energy, and vital buzz has become merely the place where I live and work. Neutral. Flat. Like everything else in my life.

The art showings I used to love have become uninteresting. The shops, unappealing. The restaurants, uninviting. After signing the contract for *Starcrossed,* I felt a flicker of excitement about the same as finding a ten-dollar bill on the sidewalk, and then… nothing.

The only real pang I get lately is when I catch the occasional early Christmas decoration. That's when I have to do my best not to flinch.

See? He ruined New York for me, he ruined Christmas, he ruined everything.

And I shouldn't be thinking about *him.*

I'm not.

But the universe begs to differ. I lift my gaze and recoil in shock. Guess I've found something worse to stare at than early Christmas decorations.

The entire window of the bookstore across the street is covered with his name. A massive bookshelf occupies the display, and on each shelf sits a tidy row of shiny copies of his new book. Riven's name is spelled out in a bold type on top of each cover like it's common for bestselling authors—red on black. Next to the shelf, a giant standee of his bust mocks me. Brown eyes stare at me with none of the warmth of the real man.

With a beating heart, I wait for the green light and cross the street. It's out of my willpower not to enter the store. I sleepwalk past the bargain books cart and head right for the new releases table where Riven's book has an honorary place in the center.

I stare at the tower of pretty hardcovers, mesmerized.

I'm not buying one.

Nu-uh.

Nope.

Riven Clark, you're not getting my hard-earned cash on top of my broken heart.

All the same, I pick up the copy sitting on top of the stack. Nothing bad in having a snoop. I flip the first few pages, title, copyright, and almost choke as I read the dedication:

To Pook, captain of my heart.

I squint at the page. What? That can't be right. He dedicated his book to me? And what does "captain of his heart" mean? Is it a sick joke? I haven't heard from him in nine months. Not a peep.

I turn the book upside-down and give it a shake as if the letters on the page could rearrange themselves and start to make sense.

They don't.

"Can I help you with anything, ma'am?" A sales assistant approaches me.

I jump, hastening to close the book. "No, thanks, I'm fine. I'll take this." I hand her the hardcover.

"Oh, wonderful choice. Riven Clark is one of my favorite authors, and this has to be his best work yet. So unexpected."

"Unexpected how?"

"I'd never imagine we'd get to see Preacher Jackson's soft side, but... well, you'll have to read it, I don't want to give away any spoilers. I could talk about Preacher and Willow for hours."

Willow? I wonder silently. I don't remember a Willow from his previous books.

After processing my payment, the clerk gives me my receipt, smiling. "Cool hair, by the way."

I stare at the pink tips of my hair. My hairdresser refused to bleach over the dye and told me my only options were to cut it off or let it grow. I've opted for a slow trimming of the pink. Half of it is gone now, and my hair has grown enough that I could cut it all off, but I haven't.

"Thanks," I mutter. I grab the book and rush out of the shop, heading straight home.

The novel weighs a ton in my bag, making me self-conscious of its presence. As I navigate the crowded streets of Manhattan, I feel judged by every stranger's eye I meet.

"Look at the sad girl, still pining after her ex," they seem to whisper.

"Stalker."

"Pathetic."

When I finally get inside my apartment, I sigh in relief as I lean against the closed door, effectively shutting the rest of the world out.

I drop my bag on the kitchen bar and ignore its contents. I shuffle out of my clothes and change into something more comfortable. Then I grab a Kit Kat out of my emergency stash. Once I'm properly sugared, I tiptoe in the open-space living room and take the book out of my bag.

I set the tome on the coffee table and sit on the couch, staring at it from a distance as if it were a nasty piece of toxic waste.

It's a staring contest I can't win.

Frustrated, I grab my phone and text Mindy.

> I've bought something

> Is it a vibrator?

> Because if you keep refusing to try dating apps, you're going to need one

I snap a picture of the incriminated book and caption it: impulse buy.

> I hope you only needed the paper to start a bonfire

> Or is it part of an exorcism ritual?

That was my initial intention

But then I saw this

I turn the first few pages and snap a pic of the dedication, captioning it: Thoughts?

Open the window and throw the book out

No, seriously, what do you think he meant by that?

Yes, seriously, trash the book

Why?

If you want to know what the dedication means, call him (you shouldn't)

If he had something to tell you, he would've reached out

That dedication is a cop-out

That man should grow a pair

Should I come over and confiscate the book?

No, I'll get rid of it

Okay

But whatever you do, don't read it

I stare at Mindy's last text, frowning... Wait a second... my thumbs fly over the virtual keyboard.

Have *you* READ it?!

The three dots appear and disappear a few times before her reply comes in.

And that's why I can help you make an informed decision

If you read it, it's going to mess with your head

You're messing with my head

And also: traitor! I'm going to block you for 24 hours

You might block me now. But then you're going to spend the night reading and unblock me the second you're finished, begging me to unscrew your mind

You're being blocked in...

3...

2...

1!

I don't actually block Mindy, but I still turn my phone off. Finally alone with my weaknesses, I grab the book and open it to chapter one.

Forty

Wendy

Ten chapters later, nothing has happened. I mean, plenty has happened. But much in line with Riven's other books: a lost treasure to recover, Preacher as the only guy on the planet who can decipher the mysterious clues to its resting place, bad guys get in the way... guns, chases, desperate circumstances... nothing out of the ordinary. Except maybe for the way the story has grabbed me. Even if I wasn't trying to find the secret answer to my failed love life in this book, I wouldn't have been able to put it down.

With a frustrated sigh, I move on to the next chapter. Unwisely, I'm thrilled when Preacher finds the panther cub and takes it with him. That was my idea. Then I curse myself for having helped Riven come up with such a good idea. With my heart in my throat, I keep reading as Preacher and Wyatt escape the tunnels and reach the missionary camp— again, my idea. But the next passage is so confusing, I have to read it twice:

> Among the chaos, a white woman hurried out of a tent. Tall, blonde, with eyes the color of the sky, she was dressed in white head to toe—white scrubs, a doctor's uniform. For a moment Preacher thought he was hallucinating, that he was having a vision of an angel descended from heaven to take them with her. Until the woman's eyebrows drew closer together and her eyes narrowed, "Who are you?" she asked, her tone not exactly welcoming.

"Preacher Jackson." Even with the extreme strain talking caused him, he took a shot at gallantry. "At your service."

The doctor stared him down, unimpressed. "You can't stay. The militia leaves this camp alone because I keep neutral. The deal is I teach the village's children and tend to the sick, but I steer clear of the conflict."

"My friend *is* sick, he's wounded."

"And past puberty by a few years, he's no innocent." Her gaze was steady as it met his. "I'm sorry, I can't help you. I can't risk the lives of all the nuns and children living here. If I help you, I'd be putting everyone else in danger."

Preacher summoned the last reserves of strength he had to argue with the stubborn woman. "You took an oath. If you turn us away, my friend will die."

She glared at him with angry blue eyes. "One night," she said. "I'll patch up your friend as best as I can and then you're on your own."

Preacher tipped his hat at her. "One night is all we need, ma'am."

"It's Willow," the woman said and then shouted something in the native tongue.

Two burly nuns appeared out of a tent carrying a stretcher.

The three women hurried to relieve him of Wyatt's weight, and Preacher was finally free to collapse onto his knees. Unfortunately, the move gave Willow an unobstructed view of the contents of his backpack.

Her eyes widened and her jaw dropped. "What's that in your backpack?"

"Panther cub," he said, removing the backpack from his shoulders. "You wouldn't happen to have some spare goat milk, would you?"

And then I re-read it a third time.

Classic enemy to lovers if you ask me, but something about the tone of the fictional interaction is nagging at me. The banter, the sass they have toward each other... It's almost as if reliving that first day I met Riven. Only in the book, the roles are reversed: he wants to stay at her camp and she's pushing him out. And Willow, she kind of looks like me and even the name...

I grab my phone and turn it back on. Before I can compose a message to Mindy, a stream of incoming texts pops up.

Wendy?

You've really blocked me!

Well, if you decide to unblock me when you reach the part of the story with Willow

Don't call me

I'm sleeping

If you're wondering if Willow is a literary version of you

Yes, she is

How do I know?

Keep reading, you'll know, too

No, you won't feel any better by the end

You'll probably just want to set fire to the book

Which is what you should've done in the first place

Nighty, night

My best friend is an insightful, annoying, smug know-it-all.

Besides her messages, a couple of notifications pop up from my mom. The first is a "missed call" text, the other is a long follow-up message.

Hi honey, I tried to call you but your phone was off. I've already spoken to Amy and Josh. I need to talk to you kids at the same time tomorrow. And since Joshua is still at school, I've set up a Zoom call for one p.m. before his first afternoon class. It's really important that you be there. I'll send a reminder by email thirty minutes prior. Please let me know if you read this message and if you can make it to the call, otherwise, I'll have to reschedule. Love, Mom

I smile at all the contradictions of the message. First, the old-fashioned epistolary style, as if Mom were still writing letters, and then the super tech Zoom call and email reminders. I fire her a quick answer that, sure, I can make the call. Then I eat another Kit Kat because… it's warranted, and go back to Riven's book.

After Willow accepts Preacher into the camp, they get inevitably stuck together, defending the precious relic, having plenty of jungle sex, and fending off the bad guys. By the time they save the day, it's clear they're in love, even if neither has declared it yet. But now that the adventure is over, they have to return to their lives. Willow is a doctor in Africa. Preacher is a treasure hunter with no fixed address. She is weary of men. He is emotionally unavailable.

Ha! Sounds familiar?

This fictional couple is the more adventurous version of Riven and me. I'm curious to see how they solve it. Preacher has just received a call about a new job in South America, and Willow is calling him out in the final reckoning.

I read on with my heart in my mouth.

"Do you love me?" Willow asked, the strain audible in the question.

"I do." Preacher bowed his head. "But sometimes love isn't enough. If the timing, the geography were different, we could see where this goes, but our lives are so complicated."

"Timing? Geography? If you talk about the weather next, you're going to officially win the prize for the lousiest breakup ever."

Despite the pain of reading my words thrown back at me, my lips curl into a smirk. The line, put like that into a story, almost seems humorous. I want to laugh and cry at the same time.

"I'm not breaking up with you," Preacher said.

"You might not be saying the words," Willow retorted, "but if you go back to your life and disappear from mine, then what's that? We can't have a relationship over satellite phones."

Well, that's slightly different from what happened in real life because Riven is not a treasure hunter and I'm not a missionary doctor in Africa... but the gist is the same. Their respective lives are pulling them apart, and if they want to be together, they have to make a conscious decision about it.

"Just go," Willow spat the word with half a sob. "I regret the day you and that stupid panther walked into my camp."

Atta girl, I'm right there with you. In the book, she stomps away heartbroken, and Preacher doesn't go after her. He leaves the camp equally dejected.

The chapter ends.

I flip the book, worried at the scant number of pages left. Me stomping away and Riven not chasing after me is basically how we left things. But in this fictional version, he added an extra chapter.

Ah, if only life were that easy. If we could just add a chapter at the end to solve all our messes.

I read on, but nothing happens. The story is ending similarly to all the other books Riven has written: with Preacher and Wyatt setting the basis for their next adventure. In Ecuador this time. I stare with trepidation at the thinning number of pages. The book is basically over and Preacher still hasn't done anything about Willow. Is he really going to leave her behind, just like that?

With less than ten pages left in the chapter and still nothing happening, I'm tempted to throw the book out the window in frustration. Mindy was so right. I should stop reading this.

Still, I turn another page.

Preacher lifted the last heavy metal box and handed it to Wyatt, who was already aboard the military cargo helicopter that was supposed to give them a ride to Addis Ababa's airport. They had a flight booked for South America in less than twenty-four hours.

Once the load was completed, his friend and partner of many adventures offered him a hand to jump aboard. Preacher was about to take it but dropped his arm at the last second.

This is it. Now he's going to realize he can't live without Willow.

"Sorry, man," Preacher said. "But I can't come, not yet... something I gotta take care of first."

Wyatt sat in the opened cargo bay, lighting a cigarette as his legs dangled in the open air. "Something or *someone?*" he asked, puffing out a cloud of smoke.

Preacher smirked and turned away, marching across the military base toward the main hangar.

Yes! My heart whoops in my chest. He's going back to her.

Preacher distracted the officer manning the desk, asking if they should carry extra parachutes for himself and Wyatt aboard the helicopter. He pointed at the equipment storage. The officer looked that way, leaving Preacher free to steal the keys for one of the Jeeps parked out front—which one, he didn't know.

"Nah, maybe you're right, Colonel," he said once the keys were securely hidden in his pocket. "Just having pre-flight jitters."

Preacher tipped his hat at the perplexed soldier and started to move away.

"Hey," the colonel called after him. "Where are you going? They're leaving in less than ten minutes!"

"I just have to pay the water bill, really quick."

Preacher slipped through the barracks and circled out to the front of the military base.

Four Jeeps were parked near the main gate, and Preacher kept his fingers crossed he'd stolen the keys to one of them. He could've asked for a ride into town with the next convoy, but Preacher Jackson had never been famous for his patience or rule-following streaks.

He walked straight to the parked vehicles as if it were his right to do so. He was wearing military-green overalls and blended in nicely with the crowd of soldiers. Plus, he'd learned that acting as if he had the right to do something often let him get away with it.

Still, hopping from Jeep to Jeep trying the ignition would look suspicious even to the most trusting soul, and the soldiers here were no fools. He waited for the coast to be clear of casual observers before he tested the first car. The key didn't work, and neither did his second attempt. But, third time's the charm... the engine of the third Jeep roared to life the second he turned the key into the ignition.

Now only one obstacle lay ahead: the guards manning the gates.

Would he be able to wangle his way back to Africa... back to her?

The End

That jerk ended the book on a cliffhanger! I can't believe it.

I throw the book clear across the room. The jacket falls off mid-flight, and the tome goes crashing against the wall to end up lying half-open, pages crumbling at weird angles on the floor.

Has Riven already written the sequel? And how did the love story end?

Will Preacher get back to Willow? What will he say when he sees her? How will they solve their logistic problems? I can't wait a whole year for his next book to come out to find out.

I stand up and pace around my living room. I'm being ridiculous. I'm not Willow and Riven isn't Preacher. Even if they get married in the next novel, it has nothing to do with us. I'm just frustrated because that's no way to end a novel. What a dick move. I'm going to spite him and not buy the next book, I swear. For real this time. I hope nobody buys it.

I open Goodreads and check what other readers have to say. Apparently, a discussion is flowing. Instead of focusing on the adventure and action in the story—which was a complete narrative arc, to be fair—everyone is bitching about the romance. Men and women have different opinions, though. Men tend to side with Preacher, complaining about how women want too much too soon and can't understand Preacher's internal struggle and the emotional wounds in his past. The women are fighting back, leaving all sorts of comments like: grow up, you have a Peter Pan complex, men should just grow a pair, a simple boo-hoo, and—my favorite—bite me.

One gal has left an all-caps review stating:

RIVEN CLARK, HEAR MY WORDS, IF PREACHER AND WILLOW DON'T GET TOGETHER IN THE NEXT BOOK, I'M NEVER GOING TO READ ANYTHING YOU WRITE EVER AGAIN AND I'M GOING TO ONE-STAR EVERYTHING YOU EVER TOUCHED.

I go back to the first review on the site which has accumulated 457 comments and scroll past the ones I've already read to stop at a long-winded rant from Aiden89.

> I don't understand why everyone is getting so worked up about Preacher wanting to take more than two minutes to decide to upend his entire life for a woman. I get it, we all want for them to end up together. But Willow sort of pressured him with a hard ultimatum, an all-or-nothing situation after just a couple of months that they knew each other.

Oh my gosh, is that what I did with Riven? Was I too black and white? I read the rest of the review.

> Relationships fail all the time, even in ideal conditions. Isn't it better if Preacher takes more time to think? That he's really sure before committing to Willow forever?

ClarissaBookLover94 that had Boo-hooed before has left a response to his question. I read the whole thread:

> **ClarissaBookLover94:** Okay, I see your point. But why does fiction always have to portray the woman as the clingy mess and the guy like the aloof, can't-touch-this hero?

> **Aiden89:** It goes the other way, too

> **ClarissaBookLover94:** Oh, really?

> **Aiden89:** Yeah, there are many fictional examples to the contrary

ClarissaBookLover94: Shoot...

Aiden89: Gone with the Wind

ClarissaBookLover94: That's a low blow

Aiden89: How about Roman Holiday then?

ClarissaBookLover94: That's a case of duty over love

Aiden89: I could even argue that Elizabeth Bennet played a little hard to get in Pride and Prejudice

ClarissaBookLover94: Oh my gosh, are you being serious right now?

Aiden89: Evidence says she turned down Mr. Darcy's first proposal

ClarissaBookLover94: Only because he asked for her hand in the most preposterous way

Aiden89: And what would be a non-preposterous way to ask you on a date?

I turn my eyes away from the screen.

Perfect.

Now even his readers are falling in love while fighting over his characters. I'm glad I've inspired the next great American novel and probably made Riven an extra load of cash.

The book is fiction and has nothing to do with us. Riven used me to have a good time while I was around and then monetized the experience, reducing it to a plot twist. My head tries to convince my heart that's how things went, but that stupid organ pulsating in my chest is having none of it.

Riven's feelings were real, my battered heart keeps screaming behind my rib cage, *you saw the way he looked at you. How crushed he was when you left.*

Then why hasn't he come looking for me?

Because you basically asked him to marry you before his divorce was even final.

So, what should I do now?

Before I can answer myself, a text from my sister jolts me out of my epiphany moment.

> **Are you joining the Zoom call or what?**

> **We're all waiting for you**

I stare around the living room, disconcerted. What time is it? I hadn't even noticed the sun had come up. Did I spend the entire night and morning reading? Shoot, and I completely forgot about the Zoom call.

> **Be there in a sec**

I text back and fire up my laptop. I search my emails for the link my mom sent, still freaked out that she'd know how to set up a Zoom call.

When I join the call, the screen is divided into a lot more squares than I expected. There's Mom, Amy, Joshua, but also Tess... Riven's sister? What's she doing on a call with my family? My eyes dart across the screen and sure enough find also little squares for Riven's brother, his father, and, in the lower right corner... BOOM! Riven himself.

Forty-one

Wendy

Oh my gosh, what is he doing here? Why is he on our call and why did no one tell me? I didn't exactly inform my family about our failed romance, only Amy, but shouldn't have someone at some point mentioned this was going to be a Christmas family vacation reunion?

I struggle hard not to let my hands fly to my hair to smooth it down. I haven't showered, I don't have a trace of makeup on my face, and I'm wearing sweats. I look like a total mess after a sleepless night, thanks to his stupid book that didn't even end properly.

Riven, on the contrary, looks as gorgeous as ever. No matter that in California it must be stupid early hours. The jerk looks fresh as a rose. Still an obnoxious morning person, uh?

Talk about facing your demons, mine is staring directly at the camera, and his dark eyes are punching a hole into my screen. I know he isn't looking at me, his gaze should be focused on some corner of his screen to do that, but I still feel like he's watching me. As if his eyes wanted to tell me something with that direct staring…

Thank you for the plot points and those few extra million copies sold?

I should tune down the snark, but seeing him again is turning my insides even more upside down, I want to kiss him, hit him, scream at him, make love to him… how can I have all these conflicting feelings for a single person?

I don't know, and my priority right now should be to appear as put-together as I can, despite what I might be feeling. So, I paste a fake smile on my face and greet everyone with a generic, "Hello, sorry for being late."

"It's no matter, dear," my mother replies while the others respond with a mix of hey, hi, hello.

Of course, my ears detect Riven's "Hey," among the noise with the precision of a radar system. His deep voice makes a shiver run down my spine and I do my best to act unaffected.

"Mom," Amy calls at this point. "I have about four minutes before the twins wake up from their nap."

Mom sighs. "All right, kids, this isn't easy for me to say and I hope you'll be happy for me and not upset…"

Whoa, Mom, talk about raising the stakes. What is she about to tell us? I tear my eyes away from Riven and concentrate on her.

"Last Christmas was really special… and even if our families weren't together for long… a connection was born."

I flush red. Did she find out about Riven and me? Is this an intervention? To do what? Will they force him to make an honest woman out of me? I doubt it since life isn't a Victorian romance novel.

"It started out as a friendship," Mom continues, and I nod along.

Where did she get the details?

"And that friendship soon flourished into something else, something precious that I thought at my age I wouldn't get to experience again."

I blink at the screen, *wait, what?*

She's talking about herself? She's in love? With whom?

Easy to figure out, considering how Riven's father is smiling like an idiot in his square.

Amy is frowning deeper than I must be myself, and asks, "Mom, what are you talking about?"

"I'm getting married," Mom blurts. "I mean, *we're* getting married." She looks to the side as if instead of on a computer screen, she could see Grant standing next to her in real life.

Then, in a movie-like moment, Grant's screen turns black as he disconnects from the call to then reappear in the same square as my mom. They hug and kiss.

The surrounding squares explode with reactions: shock, cheers, tears, whoops... I stand there, mouth gaping like an idiot, looking at the bottom right corner.

Riven is so still, for a moment I assume his feed has frozen, but then he blinks. He's doing that thing again where he stares straight at the camera, which means he can't be looking at anything that's happening on screen. Why? What's he thinking? What am *I* thinking?

The other members of our families who still retain some brain cells, as opposed to me, whose neurons have just been deep fried, follow up on the announcement with a stream of sensible questions:

How long have Mom and Grant been together?

Since the cabin. They started chatting and FaceTiming right after coming back. Soon the long calls turned into weekend visits, then longer trips and stays they rigorously kept secret from us, until Grant proposed.

See! Long distance can be done, at least for a time. And men who are in love do ask their women to marry them.

The next question is if they've already set a date for the wedding?

Yes, in a week. At their age, they know how precious time is and don't want to waste any.

A week! A week?! I'm going to see Riven in a week?

Where?

Florida for Thanksgiving weekend.

Are we going to find lodging at such short notice?

Not to worry, they've already booked plane tickets for the whole gang and we're staying in a hotel this time so everyone will have their own bedroom.

The mention of hotel bedrooms makes me almost break out in hysterics, while the questions continue.

Where are they going to live?

They haven't decided yet. They have grandkids on both coasts, so maybe they'll split their time between New York and LA.

Will they keep their houses?

No, they'll probably downsize to a smaller home and build their own love nest.

Once all the questions have been answered, my mom turns toward the camera, her lower lip quivering. "Are you kids really okay with this?"

Amy, Joshua, and I all hurry to reassure her we're super happy for her.

Mom covers her face with her hands and starts to cry.

"Mom, what's wrong?" both Amy and I ask.

"I thought you might take it as a sign of disrespect toward your father."

"No, Mom," I say. "He'd want you to be happy."

"Grant," my sister adds, "We're so happy you're going to become family."

Amy's words strike me like a bolt of lightning.

Riven's father is becoming family and, by the transitive property, Riven will be family, too, only not in the way I'd hoped. He's going to be my *stepbrother...* ha, ha, ha, isn't that *hilarious?*

Forty-two

Riven

As the call ends, I stare at the plane ticket for New York lying on my desk next to the laptop... timing, at least this once, seems to be on my side.

I have a wedding to attend, now all I need is a plus one.

Forty-three
Wendy

"I'm going to see Riven in a week and I shouldn't freak out," I chant as I pace my apartment. After the call with my mom ended, I showered and ate something other than a Kit Kat.

With extreme satisfaction, I took a pre-made dinner out of the freezer and stuck it in the microwave. To spite us both, I've refused to cook any of the delicious recipes Riven taught me at the cabin.

Exhaustion hit me soon afterward and I went to bed, pointlessly hoping to sleep off the book and the wedding announcement. But after hours of tossing under the sheets, trying not to think about Riven and only thinking about Riven, I'm still exhausted and another day has started.

That man has robbed me of sleep, of sanity, and of my natural hair color. *Monster.*

In just a few days, we're going to be face to face, for a long weekend in Florida *in a hotel.*

I move on to the next line of my motivational chanting. "I'm going to see Riven in a week and I won't sleep with him."

Yep. Not gonna happen. No after-hour cocktails, no sneaking to each other's rooms, and definitely no sharing of the same bed.

How about kisses on the beach at sunset?

Noooo, nuh, nope, nada, zero. Wendy, you're going to Florida to be a bridesmaid for your mom, and you will not have sex with the best man!

Not even goodbye forever, you-broke-my-heart sex?

Especially not intense, self-harming, goodbye forever, you-broke-my-heart sex!

What I'm going to do is pull myself together, go down there looking the best I can, and ignore Mr. Cliffhanger.

"Riven Clark, I'm so over you."

If I repeat the motto a million times, it might become true. Sooner rather than later, I hope. I'd better get used to being around him while keeping my hands and my heart in check because this wedding won't be the last time I see him. Christmas, Thanksgiving, Easter, graduations, births, weddings... with Grant in the family the Clarks will be invited to all these occasions. And, eventually, Riven will fall in love with someone with better timing and better geography than me and he'll bring her to all these functions.

Oh my gosh, I should get into a fancy dress and stroll the streets of New York in search of the new Yankee. Like Carrie Bradshaw in *Sex and The City*. For my first post-break-up meeting with Riven, I must look good, I must feel good, and I must be at the arm of the new Yankee. I don't even know if the Yankees *have* a new sexy player, but that's beside the point. Riven must think I'm completely, utterly over him.

The doorbell rings and without thinking I fling the door open assuming it's the mail.

Riven is on the other side, instead. He's as tall, dark, and handsome as ever.

And me?

I look like hell.

I feel even worse.

And I'm so not over him.

Forty-four

Riven

I stand on Wendy's doorstep, staring like an idiot. I thought I had her image engraved in my brain, but reality wipes away all fantasies.

She looks unbelievably cute in black leggings, a light gray sweatshirt, and with her hair down. It's grown back blonde, but the lower half is still pink, and she looks adorable.

Especially when she crosses her arms over her chest and wrinkles her nose in a prissy expression like now.

Wendy eyes the suitcase behind my back, and says, "I think you made a mistake; the wedding is next week *in Florida.*"

"I know, I'm not here for the wedding."

"No? What for, then?"

"Can I come in or should we do this on the landing?"

"Do what?"

"I talk, you listen… that sound okay?"

She gives me a stiff nod. But some initial resistance was to be expected.

In her living room, I take a moment to study the ambience. How subtly feminine and elegant everything is.

"So?" Wendy asks impatiently.

My focus snaps back to her. "I know you're not seeing anyone, romantically," I say.

"I've been busy with work," she replies curtly and narrows her eyes. "How do you know?"

"Your sister told me."

A shade of betrayal crosses her face. "You've been speaking to Amy?"

"Only in the last week or so, before I bought the plane ticket to New York."

"Mmm." She gives a stiff nod and then asks, "Are you going to talk, or have you come all this way to stare around my living room like an idiot."

I'm about to launch into my grand speech when my eyes land on a discarded copy of my book, lying in the far corner as if someone had hauled it at the wall. I cross the room and pick it up.

"Enjoy my latest novel?"

"I'm not a fan of cliffhangers."

"You want a spoiler on how Preacher and Willow's story ends?"

Wendy shrugs. "Not particularly."

"I'm going to tell you, anyway. Preacher is going back to the camp and beg Willow to forgive him, to take him back."

"And what about his commitment issues?"

"Preacher has had enough time to work out his past and now he's ready."

"And just like that, he expects her to overlook the hurt and the heartbreak he's put her through and forgive him."

"No, of course not. That's when Preacher will have to bring out the heavy guns. He's going to bare his heart and tell Willow he misses waking up next to her every morning, even if she's a total blanket hoarder."

"They never had blankets, they were sleeping in tents, mostly."

"And he's going to tell her he misses her lack of cooking skills."

"Willow cooked better than him."

"And most of all, he'll tell her how he misses his partner in crime. That he's realized he doesn't want to spend another day without her and that he even misses the occasional salt in his coffee."

Despite her efforts to keep a serious face, I can tell Wendy is softening up. "Willow never put salt in Preacher's coffee."

"I know, Wendy, I'm not talking about them, I'm talking about us. The truth is, I'd rather take my coffee with salt every morning if it meant you'd made it."

"And when did you realize all that?"

"The day I signed the divorce papers. When I felt sadder about not coming back home to tell you than over the end of my marriage. The timing is right this time. I've closed the door on my past and I'm certain about what I want for the future. And I'm fixing the geography issue." I take a step forward. "All my life is in that suitcase. I don't have a house, I'm not renting, and all my other stuff is in storage. I don't care where we live. If you want to stay in New York, we can live here. I can write everywhere. If you want to take it slow; I can rent an apartment in the city and we can date like regular people."

"And you won't miss the West Coast, the beach?"

"We can go to the Hamptons."

"And what about the cold?"

"I've lived in a cabin for over a year, I can manage the cold. And I'm actually excited about having seasons again."

"So, you're ready to commit. The idea of another serious relationship so soon after your divorce doesn't scare you anymore?"

"It does scare me, but it's nothing compared to the fear of living the rest of my life without you by my side."

"How am I supposed to believe you? You never even

wanted to discuss the divorce with me."

"Ask me anything, I'm an open book."

She bites on a fingernail. "This might seem trivial, but… that morning Cassie came to the cabin…"

"Yeah?" I prompt.

"You already knew she'd split up with the actor. How did you know?"

I frown, confused. I don't even remember what she's talking about.

"You mentioned an article," Wendy adds.

"Oh, that, yeah. What about it?"

"Were you still following her online while sleeping with me?"

"No, nooo," I say, as the pieces finally lock in together. "A friend from LA had forwarded me the article, that's how I knew. Wendy." I take a step forward. "That morning when you asked me all those questions, I got scared. Cassie had just left, and her visit had upset me and I thought, if my ex-wife can still get me so worked up, I'm not ready for something new. But I was wrong. The resentment I had for Cassie had nothing to do with me still having feelings for her. There's only one person I'm in love with, and it's you. I love you, Wendy. The kind of love that if you said no to me now, a cabin in the woods wouldn't be nearly remote enough, I'd have to move to Antarctica."

Wendy shakes her head, still trying to resist. "I should've never agreed to let you talk. Being good with words is your job, *literally*. How can I trust you with my heart this time?"

"Because everything we do will be on your terms. You want to date only on weekends, I can do that. You want to get married next week; I'll ask my dad if he doesn't mind having a double wedding."

"You're not being serious now."

I lock eyes with her. "I've never been more serious in my life, Wendy. I'll do anything it takes to regain your trust. The only thing I care about is knowing if I'm still in your heart, the rest, we can work out."

"Of course you're still in my heart," she finally says. "No matter how hard I tried, I haven't been able to push you out."

That's all I need to hear.

I go to her and kiss her.

When our lips touch, it's as if no time has passed at all since that last morning we made love on the cabin's couch. Only then, the passion came from a shared knowledge we were saying goodbye forever, whereas now, it spurs from the excitement of everything that lies ahead.

Infinite mornings.

Infinite nights.

Together.

Forty-five
Wendy

One Week Later

As I walk down the aisle, I can't wipe a silly, loved-up smile from my face. No, it's not my wedding. I'm only a bridesmaid. Today is Mom's day. But as my gaze meets that of the best man across the altar, the flutter in my chest is as powerful as if Riven and I were the ones getting married.

After he strong-armed his way back into my life, the world has returned in technicolor. Walking the streets of New York with Riven has made the city come back to life in my eyes. I can't wait to show him the beauty of Manhattan, which is no longer hidden under a blanket of bleakness. So much so, that I was actually sad we had to leave so soon to come to Florida for the wedding.

But being all together with our families again has been a blessing. A reminder of when we first met. We confessed everything the first night we all got to Florida since Amy and Tess were the only ones who knew already. Mom was thrilled by the news and so was Grant. And as for our brothers, being the cool dudes they are, they merely shrugged, taking in the info with a smug grin.

The wedding march starts, bringing me back to the here and now. I detach my gaze from the man of my dreams to watch my mom walk down the aisle on Joshua's arm. She's so beautiful and radiant I have to blink hard to fight back the tears. Grant isn't as successful.

By the time Mom has made it to the altar, the groom's eyes are all shiny with unshed tears.

The ceremony is sweet and romantic. The reception fun and joyous. Going back to our hotel room afterward is even better.

Since the moment Riven stepped back into my life, his all packed into a suitcase, we haven't spent a minute apart. He's moved into my apartment just as quickly as I'd moved into his cabin.

Now, Riven only waits until the room door is closed behind us to relieve me of my clothes. We leave a trail of discarded garments all the way to the bed, where we make love with a new intensity. The passion of two people who remember what it's like to lose each other, but that also share a promise it'll never happen again.

Once we're spent, I lean the side of my face on Riven's chest. "With my mom and your dad being together, do you think they'll want to spend Christmas in New York or LA?"

"Why? You'd rather have it somewhere else?"

"Actually, I'd love to return to the cabin, but I guess now it'll be too late in the season to book it." I chuckle. "Unless you want to risk another double-booking."

"Oh, well..." Riven scratches the back of his head. "I may have kind of bought the cabin."

"You bought it?" I straighten up in bed. "But you showed up on my doorstep claiming to be homeless."

"And I was," he says. "Without you, that place is only a property, you make it home."

"Why buy it then?"

"Call me sentimental... but I couldn't let it go. We met there. And if you decided not to take me back and memories were the only thing I could have of you, I wanted them all."

I frown now. "Were you really scared I would say no to you?"

"I hoped that you wouldn't, that what we had could withstand the test of time. But Cassie dragged the settlement out for so long, I wasn't sure you'd wait…"

I roll my eyes. "Yeah-ah, I know. You left me miserable for months."

"I'm sorry, but I needed to be one hundred percent sure before I came back into your life."

I reach a hand to caress his cheeks. "I know, and I'm sorry for making it so black and white for you, for not giving you enough space to—"

"It wasn't you." Riven interrupts me, tapping my nose.

"Ah, no?"

"Nope," he says, grinning. "I blame wrong timing and bad geography."

"Ha, Mr. Clark… that old line again?"

"What do you say, Pook, you want to invite the whole family to the cabin for the holidays, make another big, messy family break?"

"Yes," I say. "I would love to go home for Christmas."

Note from the Author

Dear Reader,

I hope you enjoyed reading Home for Christmas. This is the third book in the Christmas Romantic Comedy series, but it doesn't really matter if you started reading here or not, as all books in this series are complete standalones, totally unrelated to each other. Well, except that they share the same heartwarming, fuzzy holiday spirit. I hope you'll want to give the other books in the series a try as well.

Now, I'm going to go back to writing the last book in the First Comes Love series, Sweet Love and Country Roads, another enemies to lovers romcom that I'd postponed to write these three Christmas novels. I don't know, maybe I had my own Christmas ghost (a reference to A Christmas Caroline) whispering in my ear, and the holiday bug infected me. Anyway, if you've never heard of that other series of mine, First Comes Love, it has seven already published books, from enemies to lovers, neighbors to lovers, adventure, office romances, forced proximity… a little to satisfy all tastes. All books in this series, while interconnected, are standalones as well!

I'm also considering expanding this story, devoting a novel to Mindy and Danny. Something like Wendy wins a cruise for four and she and Riven invite Mindy and Danny, but they'd have to share a room. With all the sass, wouldn't that pair be explosive? How would you feel about that? And perhaps even Aiden89 and ClarissaBookLover94 deserve a shot at love. We'll see…

Now, I have to ask you a favor. If you loved my story, **please leave a review** on Goodreads, your favorite retailer's website, or wherever you like to post reviews (your blog, your Facebook wall, your bedroom wall, in a text to your best friend… a TikTok video!). Reviews are the best gift you can give to an author, and word of mouth is the most powerful means of book discovery.

Thank you for your constant support!

Camilla, x

PS. If you're wondering how the soap bar prank was accomplished, you have to cover the entire bar with transparent nail polish ;-)

Acknowledgments

Thank you, readers, for all your heartwarming messages and cool pictures and reviews. You are my tribe. Without your constant support, I wouldn't keep pushing through the blank pages.

Thank you to Rachel Gilbey for organizing the blog tour for this book and to all the book bloggers who participated. I love being part of your community.

Thank you to my street team, and to all of you who leave book reviews. They're so appreciated.

Thank you to my editors and proofreaders, Arnetta, Helen Baggott, and BBB Publishing for making my writing the best it could be.

And lastly, thank you to my family and friends for your constant encouragement.

Cover Image Credit: Created by Freepik